Best Wishes

PLATFORM 2

X

PLATFORM 2

Belinda Dean

To order additional copies of this book, contact:
Xlibris
UK TFN: 0800 0148620 (Toll Free inside the UK)
UK Local: 02036 956328 (+44 20 3695 6328 from outside the UK)
www.Xlibrispublishing.co.uk
Orders@Xlibrispublishing.co.uk
833973

Contents

PART 3

Dedicated to the memory of Stevie and for the blessings of family

ACKNOWLEDGEMENTS

I DECIDED TO write a book, taking my inspiration from the many people I have met during the course of my life but would stress that all the characters portrayed in this book are fictitious. Some of the locations are also fictitious. Thank you to all my friends and family who have supported and helped me finally get my book out there.

PROLOGUE

THE FREEZING NOVEMBER night was shaken from its deep slumber as the sound of metal, scraping on metal, vibrated through a still countryside. It echoed for miles around. Then, the explosive screams of twisted, tangled steel stopped and a moment of hushed silence filled the air, before being broken by the sound of pain. Voices could be heard from nearby homes, as lights were turned on. They were carried through the air to join the cacophony of noises coming from the embankment in the far fields. Dazed and confused, people slowly appeared at their doorways. The smell of burnt rubber and acrid smoke, blowing through the cold night breeze, drew their gaze towards the railway line, where an orange glow filled up the night sky. Some started to walk towards the source of the noise, whilst others ushered their children back to the safety of their front rooms, where it was warm and safe.

Two hundred miles north, a woman cowers in the corner of a room, sobbing, her hands covering her ears to the onslaught of abuse. The abuser towers over her.

PART 1

CHAPTER 1

Ann

Cudibrook - Scotland
12th Nov 1972
Mid-Morning

ANN WAS WORRIED about how far things had deteriorated between her and Stu. How had it happened? When had it happened? Sitting on the cosy sofa, she was mesmerised as her eldest child, Ailsa, carefully stacked colourful wooden bricks, erecting an impressive tower, before knocking it over to start again. She repeated the same process time after time. Watching Ailsa playing with the bricks was like her life; she had repeatedly built it back up, only to have it continually pulled back down.

When they had moved from Glasgow to Cudibrook, a small village a few miles away from the busy city, with their small family, it had seemed like the answer to her prayers. But this fantasy was short lived. The night before last, Stu had come home late again, from work, and stinking of booze. The dinner she had spent time and care on was, by that time, dried up and bore no resemblance to the roast dinner she had been so proud of.

They had been married only a short time with their new baby when she felt things slipping through her fingers. It was like trying to scoop water up with a sieve. They had grown up together. Gone to the same high school. They both left together, going straight into full time work at sixteen. Neither of them had chance to meet anyone else, so she supposed it was inevitable that they would end up married to each other. They had come from very different families, which were worlds apart. Losing both her parents in a car accident, at nineteen, had propelled Ann into adulthood ill-equipped to deal with life. Maybe she had become more dependent on Stu than she should have been. It had just happened. There had been no choice when it came to it; she had been forced to move in with his family as she could not afford the rent on her family home on only her small wage. Anyway, she had been in love with Stuart, so it seemed logical. At least that was what she had reasoned at the time. Stu came from a large Catholic family and their house seemed so full of excitement, full of life. It was so very different to her own home. She was an only child to strict, oppressive parents. Being taken under the wing of Stu's family had made her feel safe at a time when she was feeling so lost following the shock of losing her only family. The shine soon wore off, though. Too late in the day, she realised that living there was very different to visiting. His brothers were heavy drinkers. Back when she had been only visiting, that had seemed fun; it had been a novelty and she even enjoyed a bit of a drink herself with his sisters. It had been liberating at the time. Then she saw the darker side to drinking too much, when living in that environment full time. Fights kicked off all the time. There were arguments over who had bought what in the fridge, who had paid this bill and who had paid that. It was Ann who had pushed for her and Stu to find a place of their own. It had got her down living with the rest of his family and she disliked the effect it was having on them as a couple. They had been engaged since she had been eighteen and the most natural next step was marriage. They had gone ahead with a borrowed dress from his cousin Moira, and good will from friends. At the age of twenty, she got what she wanted - a place of their own.

Life was good for them both back then. They worked hard all week and met friends on Saturdays for a night out. When she fell pregnant, they were both thrilled. They became proud parents of a beautiful baby girl weighing in at 8lb 13ozs, a healthy weight, with a good set of lungs.

Life as a full-time mother was sometimes lonely, but she loved it. She even enjoyed playing the dutiful wife, having her husband's dinner ready for when he got in from work. They had both agreed that she should give up work and be a full-time mother and housewife when the baby came. Stu was doing well at work so it had made sense. The only shadow that ever appeared on the horizon was when Stu's family came knocking. At such times they would fall out. His brothers always brought around beer to soften Stu up, then money was asked for. He invariably said yes, but the money never got repaid. The loan generally came out of Ann's housekeeping. Having forgotten this a few days later, he would then moan when there wasn't anything more exciting than something on toast for his dinner. He had a very a short memory. The inevitable argument would then follow.

As the months went on, Stu started to go out after work with some of the lads.

'It's only a pint woman; stop moaning will you. A man is entitled to a pint at the end of a hard day, isn't he?'

It had shocked her. He had never talked to her in that way before. She suspected it was because he was spending too much time in bad company, picking up bad attitudes. Judging by what she had gathered from the conversations Stu had shared with her when coming home, some of those fellas were not particularly pleasant or respectful towards their other halves. Why was she making excuses for him she had thought? The apple had obviously not fallen far from the tree. He had gotten as bad as the rest of his family.

News came that she was expecting her second baby. He was furious. He blamed her, asking how it could have happened. Of course, he had been out on the beer. She should have picked her moment better. As if she had got pregnant all by herself. She was furious, as well as hurt, at his reaction. She had waited a few days and then picked her moment to talk to him, this time more carefully.

'We have another mouth to consider now Stu and we really need to watch our money,' she said, cautiously, waiting to gauge his reaction. The old Stu seemed to have listened and a couple of days later he shared the news that there was an opening for a foreman at a place in a village called Cudibrook.

'It will mean a few extra pounds a week and it is far enough away that my bloody lot won't be on the doorstep every other week for handouts. I've been talking to one of the fella's at work and there's a nice village school there. The air will be fresher for the wee ones. I think it will be a good move all round love,' he had reported, optimistically. She had been thrilled. A bit of the old Stu was back with her. It was only later that she had found out that he had been let go at work.

They had found a small cottage in the village. It was a little tatty but it had charm. It had a small sitting room with an old brick coal fireplace and off the back was a good size kitchen with enough space for a table. The wooden cupboards were quite old, with chips out of the doors, but a rub down, with a coat of white paint, brightened them up. Adding red and white checked curtains at the window had transformed the space completely. On the second floor, there were two small bedrooms and a bathroom. It only had a small back yard but a good size garden to the front. It was like a palace to her. The rent was cheaper than their old place too, so that had been a bonus. With the new arrival, a baby sister for Ailsa, she had been the happiest she had felt for months. Lately, however, that sinking feeling in the pit of her stomach had returned, as he had started falling back into bad ways once again. Twice in the last week he had been out drinking after work. She supposed the only consolation was that at least the rest of his family were not constantly at her door.

He was late up again this morning. Terrified that they may let him go, Ann was determined to speak to him tonight. She loved being in this village and thoughts of having to move back to Glasgow made her feel panicked. Perhaps she could pick up some haggis on the way back from the butchers, make his favourite meal with tatties. He always loved the smell of it greeting him when he came in from work. That should please him. They had to get things sorted; she just could not carry on worrying like this. Pushing her problems to the back of her mind, she told herself to stop wallowing. It would do her no good, she decided. Her mother's words came to mind *'you've made your bed. Now you have to lie in it.'* She decided she needed to get her and the girls out for some fresh air, despite the miserable looking weather.

Susan, Ann's newest bundle of joy, was sleeping happily in her pram with a full belly from her last feed. Ann threw on a couple more layers over Susan who was already wrapped up in the blanket she had lovingly knitted when she was expecting her, and a quilt for extra warmth, got Ailsa dressed in her outdoor clothes and manoeuvred the pram out into the crisp air. Clutching a letter in her hand, she pulled closed the slightly rotting wooden front door of the cottage. The letter was to her friend Amy. They hadn't seen each other, or been in touch, for such a long time. After putting the girls down last night, she had eventually made the effort to write to her. It had taken her mind off waiting for Stu to get home. It was bitterly cold out today, with strong winds which blew at Ann's coat, cutting straight through her as she made her way along the road towards the High Street. Plumes of cloud blew from her mouth, the warm breath hitting cold air, as she briskly pushed the girls in front of her. The bare branches of trees waved their skeletal arms, trying to grab dead leaves floating through the skyline. The High Street came into view as she rounded the corner. The low stoned buildings, once coloured bricks, had turned darker with age.

The village boasted only a hand full of shops. Its main street could be walked along in a matter of minutes, from one end to the other. After the chaos of Glasgow, it was a pleasant change being part of a smaller community. It meant that the children would grow up in the rolling countryside around the village, eventually going to the local school which catered for only around nineteen children - a far cry from the smoggy overcrowded City schools. It was quiet out today, probably due to the foul weather. Not even the normal chattering of bird songs could be heard. The birds were likely huddled together in their nests for warmth, she thought. Not many folk would want to leave the comfort of their firesides today.

As she arrived at the post office one of her neighbours, Betty, was in deep conversation with another woman. Ann gave her a quick nod and a smile as she picked up Ailsa from the top of the pram. It would be better to leave Susan snug and warm where she was. In any case, she was fast asleep and Ann would only be a minute. Cudibrook post office was only small and the warmth surrounded her as she pushed open the heavy door. A lovely smell of soap powder, mixed with newspaper ink, greeted her. Every shelf was filled to the brim with all sorts: washing up liquid, toys, sewing threads, newspapers, magazines, and even wool and knitting patterns. It was an Aladdin's cave, stocked to the brim with anything and everything that one may need without having to venture into the town or city. When she got to the counter at the far end of the shop, there was only an elderly gentleman in front, but the old gent was in the mood for chatting. That was the thing about small communities - there was no rushing about. People had time for you. It was exactly what

Ann loved about this village. No doubt the old gent hadn't seen anyone all day and was enjoying a chat. Ailsa was still babbling on in her own way and Ann chatted back to her. Behind the counter, Agnes looked past the old gent to catch Ann's eye and smiled, as if to say *'be with you in a minute'*. Eventually, the gentleman, having finished his conversation, turned around, gave Ailsa a broad grin, tickled her under the chin and raised his cap to Ann as he left the shop.

'Sorry to keep you waiting hen,' Agnes apologised. 'You know how it is, they love a chat these old boys.'

'It's no problem,' Ann reassured her. 'I only wanted a stamp for this letter. It must be nice for him to have someone to pass the time of day with.'

'Well, we will all be old one day and it doesn't cost anything to have a little bit of a natter and it makes us all feel better. Now then, how's the babbie doing? Are you coping alright with two young-uns?'

'Just about. It's fine. Tiring though. I'm enjoying it, even if you don't get a minute to yourself.' Ann really wasn't one to complain but she knew that Agnes would understand.

'Soon grow up, though don't they? You look back and forget the sleepless nights soon enough. Before you know it, they're teenagers. Can't get them out of bed in the mornings and don't get me started on getting them into bed at night.' Agnes reached over, stroked Ailsa's cheek and directed her next question towards the young child, 'Getting a big girl now aren't you, young Ailsa? I hope you're helping your mammy with your bonnie wee sister?'

'You are, aren't you sweetie? You love your Susie, don't you?' Ailsa smiled, nodding eagerly. She was clearly pleased to be spoken to, to be involved in the grown-ups conversation.

'Now whilst I think on. Can you let me know if there is anything from the Catalogue you want to order? You've got a wee bit saved up in the Christmas club and it's getting close to the date when you could do with letting me know.'

They had opened a book for the village Christmas club when they first arrived here a while back. Agnes had been quick to introduce the idea to her when they moved in to Cudibrook and Ann, being Ann, was just eager to please a potential new friend. Now, she was glad that she had a bit put to one side for Christmas. It would make things a lot easier.

'I was just working on the list on Saturday as it happens. There are just a couple more items I need to decide on but yes, I can let you have it by next week. Will that be alright?' Asked Ann.

'No problem hen. It's just that I like to get myself organised. Hate leaving all the orders until the last minute,' replied Agnes as she straightened a pile of greeting cards that sat in a basket on top of the counter. She stuck her tongue out towards Ailsa, pulling a funny face to go with it. Ailsa beamed at Agnes and chuckled. Ann passed her letter and coins to Agnes, who took them from her, breaking her gaze with the young child. She fixed the stamp onto the letter and placed it into a box next to her that contained an assortment of other post, ready to be collected. Thanking Agnes, Ann left the post office to brave the cold walk home.

As soon as she left the shop an icy gust caught her, nearly blowing her off her feet. She hurried to swing Ailsa back up on top of the pram but stopped mid action. Something was wrong, out of place. It was a moment before the realisation of what it was hit her. Space. Empty space where Susan should still be lying snuggled up asleep. Empty. Ann stared into the pram. Only a sheet and a thin blanket was left there. She thrust her hand deep inside and scrabbled around. Her eyes were not playing tricks on her. Susan was gone. Frantically, she whipped her head around the street, panic rising in her. There wasn't a soul to be seen. Terror gripped her in a vice as bile rose in her throat. Thoughts bounced around her mind but they wouldn't stick. Ailsa started to whimper; she was holding her too tightly.

Agnes was just turning to go and make her mid-morning cuppa, when an ungodly scream came tearing in at her from outside, nearly sending her falling over some boxes stacked near her feet.

CHAPTER 2

D. I. Ewan Edwards

Cudibrook - Scotland
12th Nov 1972
Mid-Morning

P. C EVIE Carmichael was at her desk when the call came in and she immediately went to the D. I. in charge at the station.

'An urgent call just came in Guv. It was from the post office on the High Street in Cudibrook. We've got a missing baby snatched from its pram,' she informed him.

Ewan Edwards jumped up, taking his feet off the desk they had been resting on. In one swift movement, he had grabbed his jacket from the back of his chair and made his way towards the door.

'Bloody hell. How long ago?' He barked.

'Ten or fifteen minutes at most,' she replied.

'Right. I want you with me, Carmichael. Get in touch with everyone we have in the area and put them in the picture. Make sure they pay attention to anyone out there with a baby. I want their names and addresses even if they seem legit. We can check them out at a later stage if necessary. I want every available plod on this. Meanwhile, we'll get down there and get the lay of the land.'

'Right. I'm right on it, Guv. I'll meet you downstairs.'

Evie was glad that D. I. Edwards was on duty. He had only been at Kilmarnock for a few weeks but already she had a growing respect for the man. A lot of the D. I.'s just saw the job in backwaters as an easy ride. They often sat back, leaving the foot soldiers to do the day to day policing. Edwards had already proven that he wasn't shy in getting his hands dirty. The fact that he was easy on the eye didn't do him any harm either, as far as Evie was concerned. Easily six foot two, he was well built and athletically toned. He moved in an easy manner of self-assurance, without coming over too cocky. He had very intense, but gentle, brown eyes that held your gaze when talking to you. His hair lay in thick blond curls, cut quite close to his head. He was young to be a D. I., but this didn't seem to affect the air of respect he seemed to command from fellow officers. Nobody on the force liked dealing with cases involving children. They dreaded it. But this D. I. would get the job done professionally and sensitively too.

When Agnes had heard the scream from outside, she wasn't the only person to run out to see what had happened. Several people had been drawn to the noise. People had chased up and down the high street and the surrounding lanes but to no avail. There was no sign of anybody carrying the child. It was as if she had disappeared into thin air. Meanwhile, Ann had been led back into the post office with some help by Agnes. In truth she almost had to be dragged; she wanted to be out, looking for her baby, but was in no fit state. They persuaded her it was best to wait for the police. Agnes took a frightened and bewildered Ailsa from Ann and tried to sooth her. She had clearly been frightened by her mother's distress. It seemed like hours until the police arrived at the post office. So many thoughts were racing around Ann's head and with so many people crowding around her, forcing her to drink sweet tea, she felt as though she couldn't breathe. She didn't want tea. She needed her baby. She felt light-headed. *Stu, someone has to call Stu. He should be here. He has to help find her.*

A deep voice cut through the cloud of fog that was swimming around inside her head. It was a strong, assertive voice, but gentle and calm in equal measures.

'Mrs Hopkins... Ann... I am D. I. Edwards. This is P. C. Carmichael. We are here to help find out what's happened to your daughter,' he said, reassuringly. He turned around, addressing no one in particular, but directed his next statement towards everybody gathered in the small post office. 'I know everybody here is concerned but I would be grateful if you could all please leave now, except for the post mistress. I want to talk to Mrs Hopkins on her own. Thank you all for your help, but we will take things from here.' The D. I. turned to Agnes, 'Can you take the little one over there please and keep her happy while I talk to Mrs Hopkins? Thank you.' The D. I. nodded from Agnes to Ailsa, giving Ailsa a little wink.

Agnes moved away to the front of the shop and chatted on quietly to Ailsa to distract her. The post office emptied, accompanied by hushed tones and concern, leaving just the five of them behind.

Ewan Edwards thought that the mother looked small and fragile. She was sat down on a lone wooden chair which had been placed by the counter for her to sit on. Her hands were clasped tightly in front of her lips as if deep in prayer. The look of sheer terror in her eyes was disturbing to witness. Her whole body was trembling, her knees were bouncing up and down and her breathing was erratic, only coming in short deep waves. The woman couldn't seem to get enough air into her lungs. He crouched in front of her to get her attention and gently took a firm hold of her shaking hands, guiding them away from her face. He wanted her to focus on what he was about to ask.

'Ann?'

Ann appeared not to have heard him. She just stared past him, with her large round eyes, at some area over his head.

He repeated himself. 'Ann, look at me please. We are here to help but you have to help us. First, I want you to tell me your husband's name and where he works so that we can get in touch with him and bring him down here.'

Ann moved her eyes down, slowly, to meet his. There was an intensity there but he wasn't sure she was registering what he was saying.

'What is his name, Ann? Where can we get a hold of him?' He was careful not to let the urgency of his questions seep through his calm exterior.

'It's Stu...Stuart,' she corrected herself. 'Stuart Hopkins. He works at the ceramic's factory not far from here, in the office. You have to get him now!'

The D. I. held Ann's stare and replied, 'That's what we are going to do now, Ann. We can send a car for him.'

The D. I. turned to P. C. Carmichael, to request that she deal with it, but the P. C. was already on the radio, passing on the details for the pickup of Ann's husband.

'Now Ann, do you want to tell me your baby's name, how old she is and what she was dressed in this morning?' Edwards went to take out his notebook and was talking to Ann as soothingly as he could. Ann looked at him and she grabbed at his hands, knocking the notebook to the floor. Her reply came out as a collection of manic sentences. 'Susan. Her name is Susan. Four months old. She will need feeding soon. Such a good girl but she will want her bottle soon. She likes her bottle on time. She will be hungry. She's a good baby but she will need her bottle. She may cry. She doesn't cry much, just when she's hungry. She may be getting hungry. I only slipped out for a stamp. She will need her bottle. You have to find her. She will cry if she is hungry. She will need me.' Ann abruptly stopped speaking. The pleading in her eyes went to the very core of the D. I.

'Ok Ann. It's ok. I know we have to find her but try to keep calm. Take some deep, slow breaths and concentrate on what I ask you. What was she wearing?' The D. I. left his notebook where it was. Carmichael would take notes; he would copy his up back at the station.

Ann took a deep breath and cried out in anguish. 'Keep calm? Keep calm? How can I keep calm? Someone has taken my baby!'

'Ann, we know that but the best thing you can do to help her now is to take some time to think carefully about what she was wearing.'

Her eyes were full of tears as she looked away from him. Darting her gaze from side to side, she was biting her lower lip, trying to arrange her thoughts and piece them together.

Edwards didn't try to move his hands away from her tight grip but kept his eyes focused on hers.

'She had on a white baby-grow and a white knitted cardigan.' Ann was quiet for a moment and then she looked straight into the D. I.'s eyes. 'They've taken the white blanket I knitted her and a quilt from the pram. That is good isn't it? That means that they want to keep her warm, doesn't it? Her voice was pleading for reassurance.

Keeping his voice as calm and soothing as possible, he tried to give her that reassurance. 'Ann. I'm sure whoever took your baby will want to keep her warm. We have a lot of officers out there looking for her.

Now tell me more about her. Is she fair haired? Dark haired? Or has she any hair at all? My goddaughter had very little hair until she reached her second birthday.' The D. I. was trying to inject a little bit of humour to keep Ann at ease.

'Oh, she has hair alright, lots of dark hair, with a cute little wayward curl right at the front," Ann said slowly, through her tears. A hint of a smile played at the corners of her mouth for just a moment at the thought of her daughter.

'Good. That is really good, Ann. That will help a lot.'

Edwards turned again to the P. C., whilst still keeping a tight hold of Ann's hands, 'You get all that? I want those details updating and sent out to everyone we have. Okay?'

The P. C. didn't reply, she just gave a confirming nod and went outside the shop to radio the information.

'Ann,' Edwards continued, taking a deep breath, 'Can you think of anyone that may have taken your baby? Think carefully before you answer. Anyone, anyone at all?'

Ann just looked at him, frowning with an incredulous look in her eyes, slowly moving her head from side to side.

'No! No! There's nobody. I hardly know anyone around here. We moved from Glasgow only a few weeks back, for Stu's work. We've got no family or friends here. Well, only a cousin of Stuarts. I'm only on nodding terms with the neighbours and only chat to Agnes and the local shop owners because I shop here most days. I hardly go into the town. I haven't had chance to get to know any of the other mums yet. It takes time to get to know folk. I've never been one to make friends easily. The girls keep me busy. There are no other bairns near us of the same age that I have met yet. So no, there is nobody that could possibly have any reason to take Susan. For God's sake who do you know that would take a bairn without a mother's consent that is in their right mind?' Ann gabbled out her reply in anger.

Edwards agreed with her but there were all manner of people he had come across over his time as a copper. Common sense and people did not always go together. The real reason he had asked was apparent by his next question.

'This cousin - what about them?'

'It can't be anything to do with him. He works with Stu and his wife works the other side of town at a hairdressers. It won't be anything to do with them I tell you,' Ann was adamant.

'The other thing I need to ask you is very delicate but I do have to ask the question. Is Stuart Susan's biological father?' The D. I. steadied himself for her reaction.

'Of course he is. There is nobody like that. Stuart and I have been together since school. There hasn't been anyone else for either of us!' Ann shouted defensively.

'Okay, Ann. I'm sorry. We just have to look at all angles. Your husband shouldn't be too long now. He's been informed.' The D. I. let go of Ann's hands and stood up slowly, resting a comforting hand on her shoulder.

A couple of minutes later the door burst open, hitting the wall at the side, letting a cold wind blow through with a man that looked half crazy. He nearly knocked over Agnes, who was holding Ailsa, as he pushed towards them.

'Ann! What the bloody hell is going on? Tell me they've got it wrong. Tell me the wee bairn is here.' Stuart Hopkins almost knocked the D. I. to the ground as he grabbed his wife by the wrists hauling her to her feet, 'Annie, I'm speaking to you. Tell me they have got it wrong. Tell me you didn't leave Susie outside on her own!'

Ann seemed unable to reply. She just looked at him blankly as he yelled into her face.

'Why did you do that? You stupid, stupid woman!'

Ann just carried on staring into his angry face. All the life had suddenly gone from her eyes. They looked devoid of emotion. Ann's legs went from underneath her and she collapsed into her husband's arms. Tears were running in streaks down her cheeks.

'I don't think this is the time to start laying blame Mr Hopkins. Your wife has had a shock. You both have,' reasoned D. I. Edwards.

'What the feck has it to do with you?' Stuart roared back at him.

The D. I. hated men that shouted at women, but the man was understandably in shock. He would let it go.

Stuart held Edwards gaze for a moment, staring him straight in the eye.

'Please calm down, Sir,' Edwards tried again, 'everyone is out there looking for your daughter.'

'I swear to God, you had better find who has got our Susie before I do, because if I get my hands on them, you'll be doing me for murder.'

Evie Carmichael looked over at her D. I. and they exchanged a knowing look. There was no doubt in their minds that Stuart Hopkins looked like he was very capable of that threat. He was, however, the least of their concerns. It was starting to rain. The wind was blowing into a gale. They had to find the child as soon as possible. Their only hope was that she would be inside somewhere, warm. There was no telling how safe that place may be, though.

CHAPTER 3

Alice

Cudibrook - Scotland
12th Nov 1972
2 hours earlier

ALICE HEARD THE front door close. It was the sound of Robert leaving for work. Turning back over, she pulled the covers up over her head to shut out the daylight. By staying there, it was avoiding getting up and starting the day. There had been a cup of tea left at her bedside by Robert, but it had gone cold. Alice had pretended to be asleep when he brought it to her an hour ago. They didn't really talk anymore. There was nothing left to say that had not already been said. Sitting up and throwing the covers back, she looked around the room. There was a damp patch in the far-right hand corner of the room, by the bay window. There was a crack in the window of the bay. It was only one of the small top opening windows, but it had been left and forgotten about. The light was peeping through the crack in the curtains, showing up the damaged pane of glass. Even through the small gap, Alice could see that it was another miserable, overcast November day.

Robert had gone in later than usual today. He had a late meeting and would not return until early evening, so he had decided to take part of the morning off. He had probably hoped that she would get up and start the day with him, but Alice couldn't face it. There was nothing to get up for. Alice had given up her job a year ago and had not gone back after everything that had happened in the last year. There didn't seem any point. It wasn't as if they needed the money and she certainly didn't need all those furtive whispers and pitying looks that she knew she would get. They didn't have a clue, any of them. So damned patronising the lot of them. They had all come to see her when she had had the baby, but not one of them had been to visit after the baby had died. They probably assumed that it was catching, or that she was somehow responsible for what had happened. That's what people were like, all whispering behind your back, judging you. They had no idea what it was like to lose a child. They didn't even want to try to understand; they just crossed the street when they caught sight of you. I mean, heaven forbid they would have to speak to you. It was easier to pretend they had not seen you at all. Well blow them; she didn't need any of them. Robert wasn't much better. If he said one more time '*we just have to get on with things Alice love. There is nothing we can do to change what has happened. Things are bound to get easier with time,*' she was going to bloody swing for him.

Alice sighed deeply and caught her reflection in the mirror of the dressing table that stood opposite their double bed. Well, what *used* to be their double bed. The last few weeks Alice had made it clear to Robert that she wanted her own space. His infernal snoring kept her awake most of the night and she blamed him for her tiredness. It was after a row over his snoring, a few weeks back, that he had stomped off to the spare room and that's where he now slept. Well good riddance. At least now he had stopped trying to pester her for sex. If she was honest, it was not his snoring that kept her awake: it was the same dark thoughts going around and around her head like a carousel and it was the anger that he could sleep so soundly, oblivious to her turmoil. It made her furious with him. The sight of herself in the mirror took her by surprise; she looked grey and drawn. Her roots were most definitely out of hand. They had not been coloured for about ten weeks. It had aged her. There were dark circles under her eyes which made her look gaunt; they just served as another reminder of the sleep deprivation, brought on by the weight of her recent loss. Maybe she should pop into the hair salon and see if they could fit her in. Could she stand the questions though? *'How are you, dear? Any better? You're looking a bit peaky. Have you gone back to work yet? No? Well you know best...Blah...Blah...Sympathetic look...Blah.'* No. She decided that a walk would do her good instead. Alice swung her legs over the side of the bed and slowly stood up. Her legs felt stiff. The wardrobe door creaked as she opened it and Alice pulled out a plain skirt and a pale blue blouse. Opening a drawer in the base of the wardrobe, she found a new pair of tights and her underwear. Thank the lord for the invention of the tights. She has always disliked messing about with stockings; they were an absolute pain. Grabbing everything, she went into the bathroom to get dressed. Everyone thought she was so lucky. They had fitted a new bathroom in the 1930's detached home they owned and had an electric shower put in. Not many people could boast of having a shower and it saved her lot of time. Still, those people didn't have a clue about what was most important in life.

She and Robert had lived in Cudibrook, and this house, for about five years. They had a beautiful home which a lot of people envied. It had a new kitchen, a new bathroom, both with all of the mod cons. The bedroom furniture was a beautiful Victorian set that Robert had obtained in an auction and it suited the house very well. Alice supposed she should be happy, but she wasn't. Those things were of no consequence to her at all, not anymore. She came out of the bathroom, dressed for the day, and padded her way along the fitted carpet of the landing, hesitating outside of the bedroom door at the end of the corridor. It was the smallest of three bedrooms in the house. It sat next door to her room and faced out onto the street in front of their house. Alice put her hand on the door knob and gently turned it, allowing the door to slowly fall open. Such a beautiful room. Great care had been taken to choose the right neutral colours. From where she stood, she had full view of the cream wooden cot that sat in the far left of the room. The little pink bedding was neatly made, as if waiting to be slept in. Alice felt the bile rising in her throat and the anger welling up. She slammed the door shut and ran down the stairs. Her shoes were by the front door on the rack that lay at the bottom of the stairs, as was her handbag. Slipping on the pair of flat shoes, she grabbed her heavy winter black coat from the hall stand, along with her bag and keys, and headed out. Slamming the front door closed, she took her first steps out of the house in over a week.

The day was bitingly cold. The sky was dark and overcast. The clouds parted every now and then, forced by the wind, which allowed a small glimmer of sun to peep through. It was sure to rain later, though, as the day was going to most certainly get grimmer. Alice had no idea where she was going or why she was out here on such an awful day. It had seemed like a good idea at the time. She needed to get some air. The road their house was on was part of a main road that eventually met up with the closest village to them, called Cudibrook. Their home was one of about half a dozen along this stretch of road. All the houses were slightly different in style and age and theirs was one of the newer properties on the block. Alice looked around her at the large oaks that lined the road, all naked and ugly without their leaves. Their branches were a tangle of gnarled limbs stretching into the gloom, getting contorted by the wind. The road was quite wide and at either end were fields. Alice had turned right when she left the driveway to her home. This way led to Cudibrook village centre. It was a good half an hour walk to reach it and Alice wondered if she should turn back. What was at home though? It was full of empty rooms with painful reminders. When she reached Cudibrook, she would pop into the new cafe that had opened in the summer for tourists. There wasn't likely to be anybody in there that she knew. Alice had seldom been to the village before; she usually went into one of the big towns to shop. With some luck she would get back home before the rain came. Cudibrook village was only small. There were only about half a dozen shops, including a butchers, a small supermarket, a greengrocers, a post office, a hardware shop, a chip shop and now a small coffee shop. The largest buildings were the village school, a church, a train station and that was about it.

Alice took in the landscape around her. To the left and right were open fields, flanking the houses along this stretch of road but the countryside held no beauty for her today; it was dark and depressing. There weren't many cars on the road and the only sign of life was a field containing thickly coated sheep and the odd cow further back still, in the distance. The landscape looked bleached of colour. Dirty greens and browns. Winter had well set in, leaving it bleak and lifeless except for the farm animals dotted here and there. This rolling landscape in the summer could be breath taking with the different shades of heather and green grass. Now it was a barren, lifeless place, drab and shrouded with low lying cloud. Although it was well past breakfast time Alice was not hungry but she did feel in need of a hot drink. Her feet were feeling the cold now and although there hadn't been rain today, the ground was always muddy and wet this time of year. There was no proper pavement now as Alice had passed most of the houses along this stretch and was now coming up alongside Copthorne Woods. The day was becoming even darker and gloomier as the abundance of trees stretched across the narrowing road, blocking the light out from the winter sky. There were some pines growing amongst a variety of bare branched trees and shrubs. The smell of the pine was refreshing and quite pleasant. Alice felt a little better as the freshness greeted her senses. Just around the bend, the village came into sight. She was nearly there. Alice had been unaware of how quickly the time had passed. The surroundings had seemed to blur her sense of time and she had been lost in her own thoughts. The realisation that she had been walking at least half an hour surprised her.

The cafe was the first building in the village and from it, there were bright lights pouring out into the drab day. Alice opened the door and descended a small step down into the cafe. A bell jingled above her head, bringing a man to the front of a counter from a kitchen at the far end of the space.

'Hello there. Awful day out there, been holding off raining but will not be far off I daresay. What can I get you?'

'Just a coffee please, and maybe a toasted teacake, if you have one.'

With the smell of toast wafting through from the kitchen, Alice realised that she was now a little peckish after-all. The fresh air must have given her a slight appetite.

'Take a seat anywhere you like. You may find it warmer next to the fire. Coffee and teacake won't be long.'

Alice took a seat at a table near to an open fire that was slowly burning out.

'Like me to put on another log for you? Thought I would leave it to die out as I've not had many in today, what with it being so bad.'

'Yes, thank you. That would be nice.'

The man was in his fifties, Alice guessed. He was tall and wiry, with an unruly amount of greying hair. He wore half rimmed spectacles which were perched on the end of his rather large, bulbous nose. He was wearing a pair of dark green cords with a small white and green checked shirt, with a rather ludicrous, feminine, pink apron over the top. He saw Alice looking over at him and smiled.

'Ah, it's the wives. This is usually her territory but she had a hospital appointment in Glasgow. She's due back in three quarters of an hour if the train is running on time. They usually do of course.'

'Sorry?' Alice was momentarily confused.

'I saw you taking in my rather fetching ensemble. It suits her far better than me of course,' He laughed, he was very well spoken, originally not from this part of the country she presumed. With that, he turned to the counter and went about getting her coffee and teacake.

Alice sat staring into the fire, lost in her own thoughts. The warmth of the fire was good; it felt soothing. The cheerful man brought back her coffee and teacake, placing them in front of her, then went about his business. Alice had been careful not to make eye contact with him as she wasn't in the mood for happy small talk; she was content with her own thoughts and company.

'Can I get you a refill, my dear, I see you have an empty cup?'

Alice was brought back to the present. She must have been sat there for some time because the cup was empty and cold to the touch.

'Oh. No thank you. I need to get back before the rain comes."

'Right you are. Probably wise. It could really pour down looking at that sky out there.'

Alice swiftly paid for the coffee and teacake and left before he tried to engage her in any more small talk. As she opened the door to turn right, she hesitated and glanced left. The next building housed the post office and she noticed a pram outside. An elderly gentleman was walking away from it, slowly shuffling further up the high street. Time came to a standstill. Alice's eyes were drawn towards the pram. Everything else, including the landscape, had disappeared into a mist. Apart from that pram. It was as if it had been put there to mock her. Alice took a few tentative steps towards the post office. Her breath sent plumes of smoke from her mouth as she walked towards it. When she came to where the pram was, she looked down and saw the sleeping infant. The baby was cocooned in a blanket and looked so beautiful, like her own precious daughter. The child took her breath away.

Alice felt fury surging through her at whoever had left the child out here in this bitter wind. It may be wrapped up, but that wasn't the point. A child was a gift to be treasured, not abandoned like a dog outside in the street. Anger was boiling up inside of her, threatening to explode out from her very core. It all happened so fast - a cursory glance round at the, almost deserted, street and then she found herself reaching out and lifting the sleeping child from the pram. Alice snatched the quilt that had been over the blankets and pulled it around the baby.

Alice was hurrying down the road towards the station. The old man, that had passed by earlier, had his head down and was unaware of her light footsteps passing him by. It all happened so fast. It was like she was having an outer body experience, like it wasn't her at all. It was an impulsive decision that had seemed the most natural thing in the world to do. Alice all but ran into the station. A train was stationary on platform 2 and a rather large lady was exiting one of the carriages. She practically tripped her up as she moved past her and up into the carriage. The large lady was fumbling in her handbag and seemed not to notice. Alice pulled the door closed after herself, her heart racing. The adrenaline was coursing through her body. The whistle was blown and the train pulled away. She had been so quick that the station master on the platform hadn't even noticed her as she boarded the train.

CHAPTER 4

Carol

Ripon
12th Nov 1972

CAROL DELVED THROUGH the wardrobe looking for something suitable to wear. Nothing was fitting quite as it should; there were lumps and bumps still there. Excess baby fat. She pulled out a green woollen dress, which was as old as the hills, and tried it on. It was a little snug but comfortable. At least she would have a coat over the top which would hide most of it. She threw a silk scarf around her neck which was bright, scarlet red, littered with a pattern of green leaves. Carol loved this scarf. It brought back memories of the first present Bill had ever bought her. She smiled as she remembered how nervous he had been as to whether she would like it.

'It's gorgeous, thank you!' She'd said.

'Real silk of course,' he'd said.

Carol laughed out loud at the time. It wasn't like she was a material person. Anything he had bought would have been perfect because it was from him. The trouble was that Bill always wanted the best. Back then, and even now.

He should be here, now, with her and Sophie, not out on that god-forsaken oil rig in the middle of the ocean. It wasn't as though he couldn't get work in engineering locally, he could. But it would mean a cut in salary and Bill wasn't about to do that, even if it meant he was away from home more than he would ideally like. *'Well sod him'* she thought. *'I'm done with staying at home all day being miserable. I may as well be miserable and get out and spend some of that money, or what's the point of him earning it'.* Carol knew Bill would never resent her treating herself anyway. The point was that she knew she had arranged to meet Jenny, as a way, to punish him for being away and felt a little guilty. Whenever she was with Jenny she always spent too much.

It had been such hard work the last few months on her own. Not enough sleep. Nobody to share her concerns with. Other new mums had partners coming home every night after work to, at least, share some of it all with. That was the problem. She wanted someone to share those first moments with. Their first smile. Their first giggle. If it goes on like this, she won't recognise him when he does eventually get leave. In fact, she would be eighteen and nearly leaving home, and she would turn around and say, 'who is that fella again Mum? Is it my Dad?'

It had been barely a week after she got out of the hospital with Sophie before he was off again!

Well, she was going to get out today. She would have a lovely lunch and treat herself. She took another look in the full- length mirror, applied her lippy and went to wake Sophie from her morning sleep.

CHAPTER 5

P. C. Daniel Merrick

Yorkshire
12th Nov 1972
Late Evening

IT WAS THE end of one of P. C. Daniel Merrick's first days on the job. He had finished his shift late and was driving down Bents Lane, looking forward to putting his feet up and having a hot cup of cocoa in front of a roaring fire. He was extraordinarily tired. He reckoned this was due to the different shift patterns, which he hoped he would get used to once he got into the new routine. He had just turned the corner onto the main road that would take him home to the comfort of his sofa, when the most excruciating, grating sound of metal screaming against metal hit him. It was followed by a thundering sound of reverberating thuds which seemed to vibrate along the road on which he was travelling. The sounds echoed around the surrounding countryside in stark contrast to the stillness of the cold, dark, November night. The sound must have been carried for miles around and Merrick's mind jumped to the conclusion of a possible earth tremor, or landslide. That, however, did not seem likely. Within moments, a huge fire ball with tongues of flames shot up into the night sky, lighting up the horizon with a burnt orange glow.

Merrick immediately found a wider part of the road, with a grass verge, to pull over his old Ford Cortina on. He switched off his engine, swiftly got out of the driver's door, slammed it shut and set off across the road towards the glow that was lighting up the sky. The field he needed to get to was fenced off, so he climbed over as quickly as he was able. The fence was covered in frost and small icicles hung from the wooden rungs. The temperature was extremely low tonight. He jumped down and made his way across the field as quickly as he could, his warm breath billowing out in clouds in front of him, enriching the freezing air.

Ahead of him the air was now filling with acrid smoke, which spewed up through plumes of orange and red flames. Mangled and twisted metal and debris was littered everywhere. The carriages of a train, in part, was recognisable on the track above. It looked like the engine was half off the track and the first coach had jack knifed around it. The second, third and fourth coaches had spilled down the rail embankment into the field which lay below. A fifth coach had come clear of the others and was further away. This was the line that ran between Leeds and Ripon. The train looked like it had been lifted clear from the line and thrown like a set of dice by a croupier in a casino. Smoke and diesel fumes continued to billow out, carrying with it, the smell of burning flesh. Merrick stood there, rooted to the spot, unable to make his body parts connect with his brain. His thought process said move but his body was motionless, as if frozen to the ground by the low temperature of the winter's night.

The carnage surrounding him was worse than anything he could have ever imagined. He stood there, transfixed, his breathing coming in sharp gasps; his throat felt tight and it hurt. He was aware that the diesel fumes may make it impossible to get much closer. His heart was pounding and he had pins and needles shooting down his arms but he knew he must do something. He started towards the carriage that was closest to him but away from the main wreckage and wasn't on fire. At first, his movements were jerky and wooden, like a child's wind-up toy but pretty soon his adrenaline took over and he moved forward with more urgency. Reaching the carriage, which was on its side, he noticed it had a gaping rip down the underbelly. Tentatively, he reached out to touch the wreckage to check the temperature. It was just about bearable.

He managed to clamber carefully up and over the metal wheels, using them as a lever to get a good foot hold where he could. He reached the top, which was the side of the carriage. His eyes were streaming as the acrid smoke filled up more of the air around the field. As he was now level with one of the carriage windows that had been blown out by the impact, he leaned through to see what was there. He saw a trailing arm. He almost reared away in disgust. The arm was not attached to a body.

Merrick tried to stay focused. He gingerly used what he could to climb down into the wreckage. As he neared the bottom, which was now the other side of the carriage, he slipped and came face to face with what was left of a man's head. From what remained of the man's features, Merrick could see he was only young. One eye stared back at him. It was glassy and empty and where the other eye should have been, half the boys head gone. Merrick felt sick and forced himself to turn away from the horror.

As he moved on, there were twisted, torn fangs of metal blocking his path, sticking up like the open jaws of a monster trying to snare him. This was what was left of the roof of the carriage. Strewn all around, were broken and partly dismembered bodies. Luggage was everywhere. Parts of railway seats and luggage racks were all twisted and jumbled about. Merrick could hardly move backwards or forwards, but slowly he moved this way and that, looking for any signs of life. He had only moved about eight feet in total, for what seemed like an eternity, when he caught movement and then a soft moan coming from what he thought was a woman just a little further in front of him. There was little room to move and he had to get down on his belly and make his way slowly and carefully towards where the moan had come from. As he got closer, he saw to his left there was a woman, trapped by a seat. It was obvious by the angle of her neck that it had been broken. The noise had not come from her. He heard it again, a soft moan, but it was coming from the right. He spotted another woman; she was alive. He carefully pulled himself over to her.

He had no idea how badly she was hurt. The woman was slipping in and out of consciousness. Merrick reached her and saw something moving in her arms. The woman was clutching a bundle. He had just reached her when he caught another movement. It was a quilt in the woman's arms. From between the folds a tiny hand appeared. Merrick, now in a position to move more freely, pulled the cloth further back, which revealed two tiny eyes, sparkling out into the night. It was a small baby, only a few months old. The child had a mop of curly brown hair and it opened its tiny mouth and emitted a huge cry into the night. The loudness of the cry was deafening against the silence in the carriage but it filled Merrick's heart with an indescribable feeling of joy and hope.

The sound of sirens infiltrated the deathly atmosphere of the carriage. Merrick had realised he had been holding his breath but now it felt easier to breathe. Help was coming, he just needed to get their attention before anybody tried to clamber, as he had done, into the carriage. They needed to be aware he was here and there was life. He wasn't sure how stable the carriage now was, or the interior, since he had moved some of the debris to get access to where he was. Voices, carried over the sound of sirens, made their way to him, so they must have been close by. Merrick called out in the direction they seemed to be coming from.

'Here! Inside here! We have two survivors down this end. Can you hear me?'

There was a pause, and silence from the area he had first heard the voices.

'Hello, hello, anybody down there? Anybody hear me?' A voice shouted from where Merrick had first climbed into the carriage.

Merrick shouted louder.

'Yes! Down here! Further to your right. Off- duty officer, first on the scene. I have one female, young. I'm not sure how badly injured she is but has been drifting in and out of consciousness. One baby, appears to be unharmed.'

'Right mate got it. Sit tight, we will get to you as soon as we can.'

Lots more voices appeared to have joined the first. There was a flurry of activity with orders being barked around the carriage. Merrick felt some of the tension start to leave him but he was starting to tremble as it dawned on him the gravity of the chaos going on around him. So many dead and so few survivors. What the hell had happened here?

CHAPTER 6

D. I. Ewan Edwards

Cudibrook - Scotland
12th Nov 1972
Evening

IT WAS NOW ten o'clock in the evening and Edwards was back at his desk. The events of the day had taken their toll on him and on the rest of the team at Cudibrook and Kilmarnock. There had been a press conference arranged for 9.30 in the morning. There was little more that could be done tonight. There had been the usual statements taken from all the shop owners and staff on the High Street. Information off as many people shopping that day had yet to be traced and statements obtained, but there were a few already tracked down. Door to door enquires had started and a search team, with the dogs, had started to make its way around the surrounding countryside but the dark and the rain had made it impossible for them to continue. They would have to start again at first light.

Edwards was stifling a yawn when he saw Evie approaching from across the office with a piece of paper in her hand. He could tell by the pace of her step and the look on her face that she had something he needed to hear. He liked Evie Carmichael, although she was young and eager, there was an intuition she had shown on numerous occasions that had proven invaluable. Had she been a bloke, she would not have remained a P. C. for long. Unfortunately, being a woman, she would not get the same opportunities, even though she was better at the job than a lot of the men on the force.

'Just came in, Sir, a Robert McDonald, reported his wife missing. Got home from work at around eight tonight and found the house empty.'

'That's only a couple of hours ago, hardly a missing person at this stage Evie. I take it there is more to it than that?'

'Yes, there is. His concern, Sir, is that his wife Alice hasn't been out of the house for days, in fact for weeks really. That is why he is so worried. It is totally out of character given her recent history. Apparently, she has been suffering from depression following the death of their daughter a few months back. He left home for work around mid- morning today. His wife hardly gets out of bed most days. He's very agitated Sir.'

'We need to get over there and get a statement, have a sniff around. You are obviously thinking what I'm thinking? She could have snatched the Hopkins baby! I want you with me Carmichael, as you took the call. Well spotted. As he has already spoken to you, he will be more at ease with you there as well. We need to go in softly. Don't mention the Hopkins child until I do. We need to get as much information out of him as possible without alarming him and putting him on the defensive. Find out the names of friends or family she could have gone to visit. Has she taken a car? A suitcase? We find out any information that may give us a lead.'

'Right Sir, yes. Absolutely.'

Evie knew the facts of the call would get his attention. One of the other plods would have fobbed McDonald off with the usual *there's nothing we can do at this stage, sir. Try to get some sleep. She will be back when she's ready.* That was the standard response. There had been an edge to McDonald's voice and Evie had pressed on with her questioning of him. At first, he had been reticent to mention his wife's depression but she had coaxed it out of him. Depression was just one of those taboo subjects for some people and had to be handled delicately. A smile passed Evie's lips as she hurried to meet the D. I. outside in the carpark. Delicate was not a word most of her colleagues could spell, never mind practise.

CHAPTER 7

D. I. Ewan Edwards

Cudibrook - Scotland
12th Nov 1972
Evening

THERE WAS A front light on in the bay window of the 1930's detached house. A relatively new Rover, judging from the licence plate, was parked in the driveway. Edwards thought it was a lovely house, just the sort of place he wouldn't mind having in a few years. The McDonalds' were obviously not short of a bob or two. Evie stepped in front of her D. I. and pressed the bell. Both officers gave each other a knowing look and a reassuring smile. The light came on in the hall and the door was opened by a tall, clean cut, rather sombre man, who looked to be in his early to late forties. He ushered them into the front room which was off to the left of the front door they entered by.

Evie took in the pristine appearance of the lounge. The same smell that she had detected when walking into the hallway from the front door, was in this room also. It was the smell of furniture polish and antique wood. The smell that came from old wood was unique. It had, embedded within its very structure, many years of layers of polish, lovingly applied to it by generations. The aroma took Evie back to the old Mill owner's house that her Aunt lived in when she was a child, back in Cheshire. The sofa and armchairs in this room were not as antique as the sideboard and occasional tables either side of the armchairs, but they had been chosen to compliment the old wood, whilst still looking good enough to curl up and relax in. There were two standard lamps giving light to the room, rather than the central light, which created a warm glow. That, and the crackle coming from the real fire lit in the fireplace, should have made this a pleasant room. It wasn't that it was unpleasant, it was just the sad feeling that felt overwhelming to Evie. It wasn't something she could put her finger on; it was just there.

Having made the usual introductions, Evie and the D. I. were offered a seat on the sofa, whilst Robert McDonald took a seat in one of the armchairs, with his back to the bay window. He sat on the edge of the chair, had his arms resting forwards on his knees and was clasping his hands together in front of him. He was unaware of the wringing motion he made with them, constantly rubbing them together. He was obviously very agitated and when he started to answer the questions put to him, it was even more apparent from the cracks in his voice, that this was a very worried man.

'I have the basic details here, from the report you made to my P. C. a short while ago,' started Edwards. There was a pause before the D. I.'s next question. 'Has your wife ever suffered from depression, prior to the death of your daughter, Mr McDonald?'

'No never. Absolutely not - no never,' Robert McDonald repeated. 'I wasn't convinced it was depression to be honest. One is bound to feel overwrought, even devastated by what we have both been through, but Alice took it so badly. I could understand it for a few weeks but it's been six months now. I hoped she would have been feeling better by now. It was our doctor that diagnosed her with depression and prescribed her some pills.' McDonald looked from one officer to the other before staring back at his hands. He looked mildly uncomfortable.

'Has she ever done anything like this before? Disappeared without calling you or leaving a note?' Prompted Edwards.

'No. Again! Never!'

'She hasn't taken any clothes or her tablets with her?'

'No,' Mr McDonald appeared to say this with more authority, as if he was willing the officers to believe him. 'I have been through the wardrobe and drawers. There doesn't appear to be any of her things missing. As for the tablets, they are still in the bathroom. I don't think she took them for more than a couple of weeks anyway. They were just a waste of time she said, didn't make her feel any better. Pills were not going to bring the baby…our baby…Err…Sarah,' he made a conscious effort to use the baby's name, …'They weren't going to bring Sarah back, Alice knew that as well as I did. There was no reasoning with her.'

Edwards noticed him almost flinch when using Sarah's name.

'You told P. C. Carmichael that you have rung around all of her friends and checked she isn't with any of them? Is that correct?'

'Yes. Not that there were many to ring. My wife did not have a great circle of friends. There were a couple of colleagues she would go out with occasionally from work, but she didn't go back to work after Sarah. Thought they would be judging her for what happened. She said that people didn't understand. Not that we did either to be honest. It's such a cliché when they don't have the answers to why your child just goes to sleep one night, perfectly healthy, and then is dead in the morning. 'Cot death'. No answers, just that. It's so… so impersonal.'

It was true, Evie thought. It was a dreadful thing for any parent to have to deal with. They were left with no answers.

'Please, can't some of your officer's search the surrounding fields and empty barns around here?' His eyes were pleading, 'what if she has wandered off in one of her moods and has fallen and can't get back? It's freezing out there. It isn't like her to go out. If she did, she would certainly have been back by now if she was able,' he paused for a moment, took a deep breath and tried to steady his voice, 'I'm very concerned. Even if she decided to visit someone I haven't thought about, she would surely have been back by now?' He considered his statement for a moment and then back tracked slightly. He didn't want them to fob him off with waiting 24 hours to file a missing person's report; he wanted her found now, 'but I am certain that is not the case. My wife and I were trying for eight years for a family before we got lucky with Sarah. You can imagine how extremely hard Alice has taken this all. I love my wife very much inspector and although she has not been herself of late, I am sure she wouldn't just run off.'

Evie looked at the D. I., who had, up to now, done all the questioning. Turning her attention to Mr McDonald, she tentatively asked him about other ways in which his wife's depression had manifested itself.

'The death of your daughter must have hit you both very badly; I am so sorry for your loss. Cot death, I agree, leaves so many questions and doubts for the families concerned. We, as police, try to be sympathetic in such cases. We understand the difficulty you and your wife may have had coming to terms with your grief and frustration. We have come across the anguish this sort of loss causes to the families involved. Are you able to describe any other mood changes in your wife since losing Sarah?' Evie's voice prompted him soothingly as she continued, 'for example, did she become introvert? Cry more frequently? Was she angry? Any information you can provide us with at this time may give us a clue as to her state of mind and possibly her whereabouts.'

There was silence for a minute, as McDonald seemed to think and digest Evie's words.

'All of the above. But probably mainly angry, more than anything else. That has been the greatest change in her; she is excessively short with me and on edge. When she does manage to get out of bed, she spends the day continually cleaning. My wife is an extremely attractive woman but although the house is always, almost obsessively clean and tidy, well, her own appearance doesn't seem to matter.' He looked up at this point. 'Don't get me wrong, she is always washed and tidy, but her sparkle has gone. Alice used to visit the hair salon to have her hair done and nails painted weekly. Now, well, I can't remember the last time she went. I do most of the shopping on my way home from work. There is really no place she goes any more. You must see why I am so worried.'

Edwards and Evie turned to each other. Edwards gave Evie a small smile and an almost imperceptible nod, as if to say *you're doing a good job. Carry on*.

'Has your wife been around any other children or babies since Sarah? Many women in your wife's situation react differently?'

'Good lord no! Don't think she could bear it right now. No, that is something we have both avoided. Far too painful.'

The D. I. took a deep breath after allowing a small pause and took back over.

'There is no easy way to tell you this Mr McDonald but we have to inform you that earlier today in Cudibrook Village we received a call about a missing child. The child, an infant, was taken from her pram whilst sleeping. The mother had popped into the post office and was only in there a short time. When she came back out, the child was gone. Now think very carefully before you answer my next question. Is it likely that your wife could have taken that child, given her present state of mind?'

The colour drained from the face of the man sat in the armchair opposite Edwards.

'No. Never. We have been through hell the last few months. We wouldn't wish the pain of loss on anyone else. No, no I cannot comprehend her doing that. I just can't.'

However, now this question had been put forward, despite his protests, McDonald appeared to age by ten years. He shrank back into the armchair in which he was sitting, brought his hands up towards his head and ran them through his hair and across his face; you could feel his despair.

Edwards already knew the answer to the question and hadn't needed the husband's response. His wife had possibly abducted someone else's child and he needed McDonald to understand the missing child and his missing wife were likely connected. The child was his priority.

CHAPTER 8

D. I. Ewan Edwards

Cudibrook-Scotland
13th Nov 1972
Early Afternoon

THE PRESS CONFERENCE the next morning had to be revised due to the new information. Matters would have to be handled differently to go forward with the investigation. The woman believed to have taken the child was obviously not stable. This was their only probable lead. To involve the press could make matters much worse and could possibly put the child in danger. Edwards would need to speak with Alice McDonalds' GP and try to ascertain from him what he thought her state of mind would be. He needed to get as much information as possible to guide him. Meanwhile, the husband had given them a list of any people that Alice McDonald was in contact with. Just because she had not been in touch with them yet, did not mean that she would not turn up there. He had a team of officers working through the list. Calls had been made to any hotels and B&B's within a ten mile radius. They would widen the search if need be. All train stations and bus stations had been given a description of her and the baby. The husband had supplied a photograph of his wife to help with identification.

As things turned out, it was all for nothing as Edwards took the hardest phone call of his career as a copper to date. The call was from Leeds Met. There had been a horrific train crash just outside Ripon, North Yorkshire, with fatalities. It had been all over the news channels this morning. Edwards had been so tied up with his own investigation that he had not had chance to take in the severity or details of the crash. The officer he was speaking to was part of a special team set up to contact the relatives of the deceased and get them in to positively identify, where possible, the bodies. The officer had information that led him to believe that an Alice McDonald had been on the train at the time of the accident. A purse had been found in a handbag next to the body of a woman that they now believed to be her. The other survivors were in the process of being identified. The news hit Edwards like a Sledgehammer. His mouth went dry and he could feel the bile rising in his stomach. The question as he asked it, came out as a hoarse whisper.

'Was there an infant found with her?'

'I'm afraid there was. The child didn't survive.'

'Do you know the gender of the child and approximate age?'

'Female infant, approximately between four and five months old.'

With a heavy heart, Edwards spent the next few minutes filling in the officer of the situation he was dealing with in Scotland. He supplied him with a detailed description of Susan's hair colour, eye colour and what she was wearing to ascertain if they could confirm the dead infant as their missing baby. There was silence from both ends of the line after he had finished. The silence seemed to stretch on but the officer at the other end of the line eventually spoke.

'That information appears to match the information we have here. Jesus mate, I don't envy your next job. What a nightmare for the families. Thought my job was bad but Christ almighty!' He paused, and then, 'The condition of the woman's body isn't too bad but the child's body will make identification very distressing. In fact, I will suggest that if we get a positive ID on this Mrs McDonald from the husband, then we can save the child's family any more trauma by having to come here to identify the body. It seems pretty much conclusive. We need you chaps to inform the families though, sorry mate.'

'Right you are. Can you give me a number to get back to you on? I will need to sort out what the families want to do at this stage and come back to you.' The D. I. was trying hard to keep his voice from cracking over the phone. He could not continue this call. He needed to get himself together and organise his thoughts. The officer at the other end of the line didn't press him further. He gave him a number to reach him on. The D. I. put the receiver back on the hook and looked up. Evie, who had been hovering close by, heard some of the conversation and called for hush from the other officers in the room.

'Sir, have we found them?' Evie asked in a quiet voice.

Edwards didn't trust himself to speak. His expression said it all. He just shook his head and turned his back on the squad room and headed for the gents. He only just got to the urinal before he threw up. Tears poured down his face.

CHAPTER 9

David Richards

Leeds
14th Nov 1972

'HEAD TRAUMA IS a difficult prognosis at this stage. It will be a matter of monitoring your wife's condition and then it is a waiting game. Unfortunately, there are no guarantees at this time. However, there does not appear to be any bleeding from the brain, just some swelling. We have her sedated but when we bring her round there may be an element of confusion. A probable prognosis may also be that there could be some short-term memory loss. In most cases, it will drift back in bits and pieces, much like putting the pieces of a jig saw together. The worst case scenario,' He hesitated momentarily. He didn't want to frighten Mr Woods but it was his job to ensure that he was prepared for every eventuality, 'in some instances, the patient can be left with an absence of some memories which do not come back at all.'

Bill struggle to take all of this in.

'Will she remember anything of the day of the accident?'

'It is highly unlikely at first I should imagine most things will return to her slowly over time. No guarantees though. Every head trauma can vary. We will have a better idea over the next few days. The brain is an extremely complex organ. With something like a broken leg, one can see from an x-ray where the damage has occurred. We know what to do to fix it. All I can say to you at this stage is, be patient,' he smiled sympathetically. 'That is all you can do for your wife at the moment. You may expect a degree of disorientation, mood swings and such like. We will be monitoring the situation very closely so try to relax. Your wife, believe it or not, is one of the lucky ones.'

David Richards, the consultant neurologist, took William Woods' hand in his and gave it a firm reassuring handshake, before turning on his heels and making his way quickly from the room.

The hospital had been busy the last 48 hours, mainly due to the train crash just outside of Ripon. The serious cases had been sent to his hospital, Leeds General, and Richards was particularly busy due to the large number of head traumas he was dealing with. There had been a great deal of fatalities and not many survivors. There were terrible losses for many families. The woman he had just seen, Carol Woods, was particularly lucky, and her baby even more so. The child had escaped without even a scratch. It was a miracle really. The protection of the mother's body had effectively saved her life. That, together with a quilt, not to mention the mother's thick woollen coat, had cushioned the child's small body. Carol Woods herself had sustained a fractured pelvis, a broken rib and a head injury, as well as some cuts and bruises. Not everyone in that carriage had been so lucky. The only other survivor had been an elderly gentleman, who was probably saved only by virtue of the fact that he had been intoxicated. He had been asleep at the time of impact. He had woken up in hospital with a few cuts and bruises.

As it turned out, it would need a lot of patience as Carol Woods did not regain full consciousness after the sedation wore off. They were unable to fully arouse her. She had slipped into a coma. It would be a further four plus months before she would come out of it.

CHAPTER 10

D. I. Edwards

Cudibrook-Scotland
Dec 1972

E DWARDS AND CARMICHAEL sat at the back of the church. It was an unusually sunny day for the time of year. It was a small blessing, given the depressing nature of the day. The church was packed with people. Most of them were hardly known personally to the family but this was a small village and they were grieving for one of their own. Edwards scanned the church, recognising many locals. All of the small businesses in the community had closed for the day as a mark of respect. There was a lot of the office staff from the ceramic's factory where Stuart Hopkins worked. People wanted to offer their condolences. It was always sad, the funeral of a child. It touched most people in one form or another. Edwards doubted that Alice McDonald's funeral would have a fraction of the same turn out. He felt for her husband. The whole situation had a devastating and tragic outcome for both families.

He wondered how people did it. How did you ever get over the loss of a child? The news was full of it on a weekly basis.

A couple that lost a child in a house fire.

A brother who lost a sister in a lake. The lake had seemed safe but she had got snagged by debris under the water. The brother had been unable to get to her in time.

A car accident that took a father and two twins, leaving the mother to deal with the loss of her entire family.

Somehow these people got through. How they found the strength to get up day after day and carry on was a mystery. He hoped that he would never find himself in the position to find out. They seemed to go about their daily routines. It must always be there, though, dragging them down. Those loved ones must be their first thought when they opened their eyes in the morning and the last thing in their minds before sleep would eventually claim them. Then, they would wake up and do it all again: that day, the next day and the day after that. Each year there would be inevitable anniversaries: birthdays, Christmas, the date the accident happened and the date of the funeral. He moved his head side to side lost in his thoughts. He had no idea how they did it. Jesus. This day was just the start for this poor family. Everyone in this church knew that. They were all secretly glad it was not them, not their loved ones, and he supposed by being here, they would also send up a prayer of thanks that it wasn't. The day of the funeral will be a memory that will fade for most of the people here today. But not for Ann and Stuart Hopkins. They would join the rest of the unlucky people that just about survive swimming against the storm of emotions each day.

The music signalled the arrival of the family. A tiny white coffin was carried in by Stuart. He looked like the walking dead. His face was like a Halloween mask. His eyes were red rimmed from the tears he had shed and dark shadows underneath them showed up the grey pallor of his skin. He kept his eyes trained forward toward the small alter at the front of the church.

Ann was cradling Ailsa in her arms. Like her husband, her eyes were red raw and puffy from crying, and almost certainly from lack of sleep. Yet, there was a dignity about them. Edwards had nothing but respect at the way they were dealing with this moment.

Ailsa, even, was very still. She was too young to fully understand what was happening but the child had sensed the gravity of the situation. With any luck, she would forget more easily than her parents, being so young. Children had a knack of bouncing back far more easily than adults.

Stuart placed the little coffin on a small table in front of the church alter which was surrounded with flowers and teddy bears. On top of the coffin lid, was the white blanket Edwards had handed back to Ann after he had received it from the Northern team of investigators. This was all she had left of her baby. He had only decided to pass it on to her because there was miraculously no evidence of her child's tragic death. It was one of the hardest times he had endured during this investigation. He remembered how she had taken it gently from his hand as if it were made of glass. She had drawn it to her nose and closed her eyes breathing in.

'It doesn't smell of her, it smells of smoke and petrol. Why doesn't it smell of her? It should smell of her,' she had dropped to her knees and wailed like an injured animal.

He had sat with her for half an hour trying to comfort her. He hadn't meant to bring her more pain. Where her bloody husband was, God only knew. He should have been there. It was early evening so he couldn't have been at work. Eventually, she had calmed down and taken it to the sink to put in a bowl with some soapy water.

'Thank you,' she had said as she showed him to the door.

The service didn't take long. The vicar was obviously aware that he needed to make the service as swift and painless as possible. All the right things, that the occasion demanded, had been said by him. The usual platitudes of God's love and finding faith and hope in his everlasting love but everyone in the congregation must have all felt as he himself did, that the words would not mean a damn thing, or be of much comfort to Ann and Stuart at this time.

After the service, the couple walked away from the church amongst hushed offers of sympathy and support. It was clear that they were in their own world of torment and they just kept their heads high. Their eyes were empty, uncomprehending of the words spoken to them. Stuart had his arm around his wife in case her legs abandoned her during the short walk to their home, only a few minutes away from the church. Edwards had offered to drive them the short way but they had politely declined. His face was probably the last face the couple wanted to see and he understood their need to just go home and shut the door to the world outside. They needed to get through this day in their own way. God help them.

Then there was Robert McDonald dealing with his own anguish. The funeral of his wife was further afield, some twenty miles away, out of respect for the Hopkins. He had told the officers that he would go and stay with his sister in Southampton, leaving immediately after the funeral. He was intending to put his house in the hands of a local agent. There was nothing left for him in Cudibrook; he didn't wish to remain there and add to the grief of the Hopkins family. McDonald had his own demons to deal with. Although he was angry about his wife's actions, he had loved her - she had been his whole life. But Alice was gone now and he was still here. He was angry with himself for not recognising how very disturbed and unhappy she had become. He had said that he would never be able to forgive himself for letting her down and what that had led to. The D. I. felt bad for him. He had seemed a decent sort of bloke. He also understood why he felt he could not stay around this area. It was really a relief to Ewan. He didn't want to be called out in the future because Stuart Hopkins or anybody else had gone seeking revenge.

The D. I. sensed that Stuart Hopkins may have to be watched. From what he could gather, the man drank far too much. Alcohol and grief could be a dangerous combination, although having seen him today, he didn't look capable of very much at all. He looked a broken man. There were times, like the past couple of weeks, that Ewan Edwards wondered why the hell he was in this job.

CHAPTER II

Carol

Leeds
March 1973

CAROL WAS SORE: her joints were stiff; she was groggy and disorientated; her throat was painful and her mouth and lips were dry, sore and cracked. She had come around in the early hours of the morning. Doctors had made some assessments and called her family to be with her. They were at her bedside as soon as they had been given permission to see her. Bill, who had popped out for some teas, had looked so relieved when she had opened her eyes and spoken his name. Carol had no memory of the accident. Details of what had happened had been filled in for her. Her mother had tight hold of one of her hands.

'I can't believe you were out of it for so long. I would never have forgiven myself if I had lost you. It certainly puts things into perspective. That hotel takes all my time and I never get to see you. I have been very remiss. Yes, very remiss. Oh dear. Well, I am here now my love and Joe can keep things ticking over with the hotel. I'm here for as long as you need me.'

Carol had groaned inwardly.

They had not had the closet mother-daughter relationship when she was growing up, or for as long as she could remember. Her mother had always been involved in numerous community projects and was always too busy with her various hobbies to spend time with her daughter. Her friends' mums seemed warmer and cosier. Her mother, Jane, was a little highly strung and excitable, even a little self-absorbed. Often, she forgot Carol's parents' evenings and if she did remember, got the wrong time and seemed far more interested in relaying her conversations with the other parents than letting Carol know how the teacher felt she was doing in school.

Carol guessed she had done her best, considering she had been left a widow quite early on. Carol's father had died from a stroke at the age of forty-one and Carol's memory was of a rather starchy accountant. He was of the generation that children should be seen and not heard. Her mother had always been a volunteer in some charity shop or other from Carol being young and had spent a lot of time being cared for by her grandmother. Perhaps that was why Carol was so independent. She presumed that Carol did not need her and left her to get on with her life whilst her mother got on with hers. Her parents had not produced any siblings for Carol, so she was an only child.

When Carol had been expecting her first baby, her mother kept on promising to come and see her. It never happened. Carol's husband, Bill, had a job that took him away, sometimes for weeks on end as he worked on the Riggs. When the baby was due mid-July, again Carol's mother, Jane, promised to come to stay and help with the baby. But then two weeks before the baby was due, Bill got shore leave and Jane said she would wait until the baby arrived and come and stay when Bill had gone back to the rig.

As it turned out, she had to cope practically single handed. Bill was back on the Riggs a week after their baby arrived and this was the first time she had seen him since. He had been gone for over three and a half months. It wasn't the greatest way to have to get your husband's attention.

'Family bonding time, darling, that's what you need. Let Bill get involved with the baby. Your father was hopeless, God rest him. Things are different these days, with your generation. It's all the rage for dads to be involved right from the word go.'

When Bill went back, there were other excuses for Jane not to visit, like some crisis or other with the B&B. Carol had long since learned not to get too disappointed. Carol smiled. It was just her mum and she loved her. It was just the way she was. It had been a long time since she judged her for her lack of motherly warmth and fuss.

Her granny had been the one that Carol had been close to. Carol was determined that she would lavish lots of love and cuddles on her new baby. Bill had been tactile with open demonstrations of affection. Well at least when he was around. That was the way Carol was determined to be with her daughter. It wasn't enough just to say I love you - it had to be shown with cuddles. It was a good job her mother had made her independent. Bill working away had seemed like a great opportunity to buy their first home. Carol had hoped that when she had had the baby, he would do shorter stints. However, he was worried the work would dry up, so he said he wanted to get a bit behind them. It had got her down, as no matter how independent she was, she had found it hard on her own. The path of romance sometimes didn't always run the way she would have liked it to.

Her mother, however, seemed to do alright for herself. She met Joe, her second husband, at a local dance one of the neighbours had dragged her to. They were a very unusual combination. Joe was outgoing and quite loud, whilst Jane was rather prim; it had been a surprisingly good match. They were married quite soon after and had decided to up sticks from Yorkshire and open a B&B in Devon. Carol was dragged off to Devon but spent most of her school holidays with her grandmother, whom she adored. Jane was so busy with the business that she seemed not to miss her daughter. It made Carol smile inwardly hearing her mother refer to the B&B as a hotel. Some things never changed, she thought.

'You're here now, Mum, which I'm grateful for. He must have been struggling with her.'

'Oh, you know I love Bill. He is a darling boy but he was completely hopeless, at first.'

'He would be wouldn't he? He hasn't had any practice, seeing as he was off on his toes after I had only been home for a week. I made it look too easy.'

The doctors were talking to Carol about going home in a couple of weeks after some treatment to help her get her legs and other stiff joints moving and she couldn't wait. The thought of Sophie being there waiting for her was all she needed to make a recovery. There was a hammering in her head but the pain killers would deal with that. All she wanted right now was to hold her daughter. Carol tired easily and must have fallen asleep whilst Bill and her mother had been there. When she had woken up, she was alone.

CHAPTER 12

Ann

Cudibrook - Scotland
1976

ANN WAS SAT at the kitchen table, on her own, waiting for Stuart to come home. She felt isolated and sick to her stomach. It was nearly nine o'clock at night and Ailsa had been in bed for a good hour already. She was filled with dread, as she heard the familiar squeak of the un-oiled gate open. Ann took a deep breath and got up to get his dinner from the oven. The key turned in the lock. Ann could smell him before he even sat down; her stomach turned.

'You're late tonight. I don't know how edible your dinner will be. It's been in the oven for two hours. I will just get it for you.'

Before Ann had barely had chance to get across to the other side of the kitchen, Stuart, who had sat himself down at the kitchen table, had jumped up, and brought his right hand underneath it, throwing it over onto its side. Ann just stood there, frozen.

'Why can't you just shut your mouth? The minute I get in, you bloody start with your comments.'

Ann just looked at him. His red face was twisted in anger.

'I only said it may not be fit to eat and it probably won't be. What do you want from me Stuart? I never know when you are going to be home,' Ann almost whispered the statement.

'That's exactly what I mean - you just do not know when to shut the hell up, do you?'

Stuart lunged across the kitchen and struck Ann across the right side of her face with the back of his hand. Ann was knocked into the side of the cooker; she lost her balance and fell over onto her back, catching her left arm under her. She felt her wrist twist and the pain was intense as she hit the floor. He went totally berserk, sweeping his arms across the work surfaces, breaking cups, plates and anything he could get his hands on. All the time, he was screaming and raging at her. Twice, he came over and pulled at her from the neck of her dress, trying to get her up, but she was afraid that if he got her to her feet, then he would knock her down again just as quickly, so she tried to stay scrunched up and remain a dead weight.

Ann cowered on the floor, not daring to move or look up, frozen in terror. He came at her again and tried to drag her up. Again, she resisted, so he dropped her and kicked out, instead. He struck her in the back with his foot, knocking the wind out of her. Eventually, he stopped and all she could hear was his ragged breath panting.

'I'm going back out again for some peace and bloody quiet and when I get back this lot had bloody well better be cleared up. Don't bother with food, you only feed me shite anyway.'

Ann still did not dare move; she heard the door slam and the gate squeak telling her he had gone.

It was some minutes before she could catch her breath and steady her pounding heart. She wasn't sure she could move. She had no idea how long she had been crouched on the floor for. Slowly, she looked around at the devastation in the kitchen. She felt numb and in shock.

Ailsa was bound to have woken up with all the noise and she didn't want her to see this mess. Ann slowly tried to get up but felt a burning pain through the wrist that she had fallen on. Using her other arm, she got to her feet and gingerly, on shaky legs, making her way to the kitchen door. She held her breath and listened for sounds of her daughter. All appeared to be quiet. How that hadn't woken her, she didn't know. *Better to check on her in a minute*, she thought.

Looking around the kitchen, she couldn't believe the damage Stuart had done. He was bloody mad. Although, Ann knew that to say anything at all to him would provoke him but had done so anyway. She was stupid.

He was becoming increasingly confrontational and aggressive over the slightest thing. Why had she done that? Why? Had she expected that reaction, though? Maybe for him to raise his voice, shout even, but to hit her like that and do all this damage - it was crazy. It wasn't the first time he had lashed out. There had been a few incidents recently: shove here; a shove there; something thrown; an arm grabbed or a hand lashed out. Not this bad though - no - never as bad as this.

Ann picked up pieces of the broken crockery and tried to tidy the mess but her wrist was throbbing painfully. She went into the front room to look in the mirror above the fireplace. Her cheek was starting to throb and the numbness she first felt was giving way to more pain and her eye felt as if it were swelling and closing. When she looked at herself in the mirror, she was shocked. Her eyes filled with tears of anger and despair.

There was a knock on the front door and Ann felt a current of anxiety shoot through her. She held her breath and waited, hoping whoever it was would go away. Another knock came a minute later and then a voice shouted her.

Mrs Hopkins... Mrs Hopkins, are you there? Can you open the door please?'

Ann didn't know what to do. She was petrified to be seen in this state. She went to the door.

'Hello, who is that? It's very late. I was just in bed,' she managed to force out; her voice felt shaky but she tried to sound confident.

'It's the police, Mrs Hopkins, can I come in please?'

'Why? Is there something wrong? It really is late,' she insisted.

'Yes Mrs Hopkins, but I am not going away, so please can you let me in so we can talk a little more privately.'

She felt mortified but turned the latch with her good hand and wrist and opened the door. The sight of Evie Carmichael on the other side of the door crumbled her resolve to be in control. Ann felt the tears come and all the misery start to fall away. The door was opened wider to allow the P. C. to enter.

'I am not going to ask if you are alright, as it is obvious that you're not. Let's go through to the kitchen and have a chat,' Evie said, gently.

Ann just followed Evie like a guest in her own home, like a good puppy following its master into her own kitchen. Evie looked around at the mess and then at Ann, who stood there, looking around her blankly.

'I take it that Stuart did this?'

Ann just nodded.

'Right well first of all, let's get this table back the right way up and we can put the kettle on and have a brew and a chat.'

Evie set about getting the table upright and busied herself putting the kettle on to boil. As it was boiling, both women worked side by side picking up broken cups, plates, and other items which had been thrown around the kitchen. Then they sat at the table with tea in their hand, like two ordinary friends. Evie let the silence sit between them, whilst they sipped their tea for a few minutes.

'The way I see it, you need to get that wrist looked at and checked out at the hospital. You look a mess, Ann, to be honest. Has he done this before?' Ann did not get chance to reply before Evie continued, 'I'm guessing he has. Men don't go this far in a one-off assault. It takes time to work up to this magnitude of an attack.'

'How did you know? Did someone call you? Because it was my fault. I knew I would say something to make him lose his temper. I should have just kept quiet. It's not like I don't know I make him angry these days,' Ann uttered, miserably.

'It was just a coincidence that I was near. I heard something and saw Stuart storming up the lane, looking angry. How you can take responsibility for this is beyond me, Ann. There is no excuse for his behaviour.'

'No, but he had been drinking. I shouldn't have goaded him. I know he can get laree in drink. Most men do. Stu is under a lot of pressure, still grieving. It is his way of coping. Drinking I mean,' Ann tried to reason. Although, she felt more like she was trying to convince herself, rather than P. C. Carmichael.

'Ann you're making bloody excuses for him! Deep down, I know you agree with me. No matter how badly he feels, he has no right to take it out on you. How is he with Ailsa?'

Ann reeled, 'He has never laid a hand on Ailsa. He wouldn't, he loves her. There is absolutely no way.' Ann was horrified at the suggestion that she would ever let him near their daughter if she thought for one second that he was a threat to her, well....

'You can't know that Ann. I am sure you never thought when he first started getting abusive, that it would end up as bad as this. The answer is that you cannot be sure of anything if a man is on such a short fuse. You cannot take that risk, Ann.'

'I honestly don't think he would touch her. It is me who he blames.'

Evie narrowed her eyes in momentary confusion, 'Blames you for what, Ann?' But then, sickeningly, before Ann had chance to respond, it dawned on her.

'For losing Susan. It was my fault. Don't you see? I left her outside the post office. It was me, not Ailsa, not him, but me. It was my fault.'

Evie daren't let on that she had realised that this was what Ann had meant because it was just ludicrous, and she needed to make that clear.

'That is utter bollocks, Ann. I'm sorry to swear but it is. You weren't to blame. Nobody was to blame other than the woman who took your child. It was a tragic set of events but you cannot allow yourself to carry that burden of responsibility - it will destroy you. I am not convinced that Stu even thinks that and, if he has said it, it is bloody well out of order. He is an angry man with a temper and losing Susan or not losing Susan, he would most probably be angry about something. We can all use excuses for bad behaviour but the bottom line is, there is no excuse for what he has done here. You should let me pick him up and you should press charges. He's out of control, Ann.'

'No, I can't do that! I just can't. I will make it work with him. I will try harder. I have to. There is no other way.'

'I'm sorry, Ann, but I think you're wrong here,' her eyes pleaded with Ann to see sense but she knew that she was fighting a losing battle. Ann was determined to make things work with her husband, 'well, I guess I can't force you. Have you talked to anybody about this, a friend perhaps?'

'God no. I would die of embarrassment. No, I can handle it. It just got out of hand. It will be fine, I promise.'

'Well, I really wish you would at least let me pick him up and have a word with him. Let him know that we know what he has done, even if you will not take it any further.'

'No. It will make it worse. I can handle it, I promise. He would never touch Ailsa. I know he wouldn't.'

'It's your call. I will leave my card for you. Call anytime if you want to talk again or change your mind but I am going to pop round from time to time. I need to see for myself that you and Ailsa are alright, okay?'

'Okay then,' Ann said, secretly relieved.

Evie left her card on the table and Ann let her show herself out.

Ann felt so embarrassed. The neighbours must have called the police. It was too convenient that Evie was just passing; they must have heard Stuart. Ann got up and went upstairs to run a warm bath, clean her-self up and check on Ailsa. She popped her head around the door. Ailsa was fast asleep, curled up in the foetal position, hugging her favourite brown bear. The movement made her head bang and she felt sick. She was so tired and so hopeless. How she longed not to wake up tomorrow, but what choice did she have, there was Ailsa to think about and she loved her so much. At this very moment she hated Stu and wished to God he would just disappear. How could things have gotten so bad? Where had the young optimistic young teenagers gone? They had been so in love once, she was sure, but it seemed so long ago now.

After gently soaping her sore body, she towelled herself off, threw a thick cotton nightdress on and fell into bed, exhausted. She lay there at first, her ears straining for the slightest noise coming from downstairs to announce his return. With every small sound from outside, she could feel herself tensing and holding her breath. She listened for his familiar footsteps but eventually, exhaustion took over and Ann fell into a heavy sleep.

Stuart did not come home that night. In fact, he didn't come home until the following Monday. After the first two nights of him not coming home, Ann didn't prepare food for him. She felt relief at him not being there and Ailsa only asked once in passing where her daddy was. She just told her that he had gone away with work and wasn't quite sure when he would be back. Ailsa seemed satisfied with the lie.

On the Monday Ann's gut twisted when she heard the familiar squeak from the gate and then the key in the lock. He came straight through to the kitchen.

'I've had a pie at the pub, so you don't need to cook,' he announced on arrival.

'Well that's good because I haven't. Thought you had left as I haven't seen sight nor sound of you for the last few days and please don't raise your voice, Ailsa is in her bedroom playing.'

'I wasn't going to. Why do you make out like I am the one at fault? You know you provoked me Ann, I just want to come home to a decent meal without your attitude.'

'Well then we both want the same thing. I want to provide that meal but I never know when you are here. We can't go on like this, Stuart. I don't know what time you are in or even if you are coming home at all.'

'I am always home but I will not clock in and out in my own bloody house. I was dammed if I wanted to come home the last few days. If you must know, it's because I chose not to listen to your damn nagging. I will come and go as I bloody well please.'

'You're starting to shout again. Can you please not do that? I cannot cook if I do not know when, or if, you are coming home. That seems reasonable to me.'

'Don't tell me not to shout in my own home, woman. You see there you go again, goading me!'

'I am not trying to goad you Stuart, I just need to know when to cook and when not to.'

'Oh for God's sake! Don't bloody bother to cook me anything then if it stops your whining. I will eat at the canteen at work and grab something on my way home. Stop you interrogating me, then. Jesus, I just want some peace.'

'What do I want Stu? Have you ever thought about what I want? Where have you been the last few days? Surely, as your wife and the mother of your child, I am entitled to know.'

'You've got what you want, haven't you? A home, a child, food on the table - which I provide for you, I might add. You are not entitled to ask me anything but if you must know, I slept on a mate's couch and now I am going out again, after I have changed and had a bath. I may or may not come home. I may stay at my mate's house again. I'll decide that later,' and with that, he stormed out of the kitchen and up the stairs.

Well at least there was no cooking to do for him and he hadn't thumped her. Ann supposed she should be grateful for small mercies. She still felt sick, though. She was unaware that she had been holding herself tightly, waiting for him to go off on one again. But she was proud she had been firm when all she really wanted to do was cower away and hide. Ann heard him bang the bathroom door shut. With any luck, he would be out again within the hour. He hadn't even apologised for hurting her. He had not actually looked at her at all, she realised. Throughout the whole conversation, he had been half turned away. He just didn't care about her or Ailsa anymore. He had not even gone in to speak to his daughter who was playing in her bedroom but had gone straight to the bathroom, instead. She found that she had tears rolling down her face. *What happened to us,* she whispered, more to herself than Stuart. Annoyed at her own weakness, she brushed them away, angrily. Turning to the stove, she made herself a cup of tea and went into the lounge and switched on the T.V. It was less than half an hour later when she heard the front door slam.

'Mummy? Was that Daddy?' Ailsa was stood in the doorway.

'Yes sweetie, but he has gone out again. Are you ready for your tea? It's just you and me again tonight,' she chirped at her daughter, plastering on a smile. It was only half faked.

'Yes please! Can we have cheesy worms tonight? I love cheesy worms. Daddy doesn't like cheesy worms, but we do, don't we, Mummy?'

Cheesy worms were what Ailsa called macaroni with cheese. Ann had made up all sorts of funny names for food when Ailsa was little to make food more fun.

'We certainly do honey and we can have what we want, can't we? If Daddy isn't here. Do you miss Daddy sweetie?'

Ailsa paused and pulled an exaggerated, thoughtful face. This was typical of Ailsa - so dramatic and theatrical.

'Well, not really Mummy. I don't like it when I hear Daddy being shouty. It makes my tummy all squiggly and we can have cheesy worms can't we? if he isn't here, and that's good, isn't it?'

'Yes, sweetie. It is. But aren't you a bit sad Daddy isn't here?'

'No, Mummy. I think it is Daddy who is sad.'

'Why, honey?'

'Because he always seems so cross!'

Ann was shocked that her daughter was so intuitive and also sad that she had a *squiggly tummy*, as she put it. Ann had not realised that her daughter had noticed Stuarts growing moods but she obviously had. Maybe it was better if he wasn't here but when he was, there had to be a way of making things better, she just didn't know how. Ann got up and followed her daughter to the kitchen to make the tea. Just the two of them tonight, thought Ann, but at least a peaceful meal.

Ann had dropped into an exhausted sleep but was woken when she felt Stuart climb into bed next to her. He stunk of drink and perfume. Not for the first time, she wondered if he was seeing someone else. The weird thing was, that she rather hoped in some ways that he was. It would mean that he would not roll over to her in the night and go through any pretence of affection for a prelude to sex. Sex had never normally been an issue for them. Their sex life had always been good, to a degree, up until they lost Susan. Even with the tiredness that comes from having small children and sleepless nights, they had had a fairly regular sex life. Stuart had always been considerate in that department and had a gentle side of his nature. Lying next to him now, Ann wondered if that had been a different man. She herself had certainly changed towards him, but it was difficult to determine, at exactly what point, they had drifted to this stage. Grief and blame had of course brought them to this point. There was no fooling herself that was when things escalated. His anger towards her that first evening Susie had been taken. It made her stomach lurch even now thinking back. Each of them had reacted so differently. It was like living with a stranger. There was no doubt he blamed her for the loss of their child.

Stuart soon snored his way into a drunken sleep, whilst she was still wide awake. Quietly, she slipped out of bed and pulled her cardigan from the chair at the side of the bed. Throwing it around her shoulders and slipping into her slippers, she made her way, silently, around the bed and out through the bedroom door. There was no way he would wake up, even if she had stomped her way across to the door; he was in a deep, drunken sleep.

Ann crept over the landing to her daughter's room and stood in the doorway looking down at her snuggled down under her covers. Ailsa's hair was plaited each night before bed but little wisps of tiny curls had escaped and formed a halo around her little face. Ann could not believe how beautiful and perfect her child was. Thoughts flashed into her mind of another little face that should have been sharing this room. It did not seem like four years since Susan was taken. Sometimes, it seemed like only yesterday. Other times, it felt like much longer than four years, even like she had never even existed. Ailsa always slept with a small lamp on in her room. She, like most young children, didn't like the dark. Ann took a last look at her sleeping child and made her way downstairs and through to the kitchen.

The clock hanging on the kitchen wall told Ann that it was 2.40 am. Surely there was no way Stuart had been in the pub till this time. There was no way, either, that Ann was going to question him. There was no doubt in her mind that he was going somewhere else. He should just go there. It was not like there was much for him here. He took no notice of Ailsa, and Ann just seemed to anger him. She put some milk in a pan to boil. Cocoa was comforting and she felt in need of comfort. It was as she was sat, sipping her drink, that she heard a light rap on the kitchen door. The kitchen door opened onto a garden at the side of the property.

Ann got up and quietly asked, 'Who is it?'

An equally quiet voice returned, 'It's just Evie. I saw your light on as I was doing my rounds. Are you OK?'

Ann unlocked the door, opened it and beckoned Evie in.

'Come in, it's freezing out there. I'll make you a hot drink.'

Ann made her way towards the stove, paused a moment, slowly turned to face Evie and sighed, 'It depends on what you mean by OK. Stuart's home tonight and dead to the world, thanks to the amount of beer he must have drunk. I was just down here having a cup of cocoa. I find it calms me. Want one?'

'I'd prefer tea, if that's OK? So how have things been? Have you thought any more about what we talked about last week?'

Ann reached up into a cupboard above her head. She brought back down a pack of tea bags to replenish the jar that sat on the counter top, 'I have thought of nothing else. I think of the way things used to be and then I think of the way things are now. He only came back tonight. He stayed just long enough to wash and change and go back out again but at least he controlled his temper. It is early days, Evie.'

'Too ashamed to face you more like. Men like Stuart cannot face up to the damage they cause. They act like it has nothing to do with them. What about the next time? And the time after that, Ann? You have to be a realist. You cannot live like this.'

'It's easy to say the words, Evie,' she hands her, her cup of tea, 'but I have a child and she needs a home. Where would I go? I have no family and Stuart's family are a non-starter. I have no job, no independence. Apart from that, he's my husband and I am his wife. He's Ailsa's father, I need to try to work through this. It wasn't always like this between us both. We used to be good together, believe it or not.' She puts the milk back in the fridge and returns to the table.

'Get a part time job. There are always bits of work here and there, if you want it. Ailsa is at school now and you can work around her school times. At least then it would give you a little independence from Stuart.'

'I'm already a step ahead of you on that one. The rent is in arrears by a month and my housekeeping gets less each week. I don't think I have any choice in the matter but I need to have that discussion with Stuart. On the one hand, I'm dreading it, but on the other hand, it has got to be done sooner than later. I just have to pick my moment. I don't think he cares what I do to be honest. At one time he would not hear of me going out to work, but now, well, I don't think it will bother him,' she aimlessly stirs a spoon in her cocoa, 'I just cannot call what his reaction will be.'

'You shouldn't even be worried about having that conversation, Ann. That is exactly what I am talking about. You cannot live in fear.' At this point, having forgotten about the tea in front of her, Evie takes a giant gulp of the, now nearly cold, drink.

'I know Evie, but just let me deal with this. I am sure that if we work at it, we can turn things around. Extra money coming in will be a start, I'm sure.'

After Evie had left, Ann felt exhausted again. Evie made it all sound so simple but it wasn't. Ann knew that she'd have to get a job, especially now she knew she could no longer rely on Stuart. He was just no longer the man she had married. She wasn't even sure that man was there anymore. Even if she could find him, would things ever be comfortable between them again?

Ann curled up on the sofa under a woollen blanket. She had a lot of thinking to do.

Ann was woken up by her daughter running down the stairs and demanding hot cornflakes. Ann, having dressed and given her daughter breakfast, went up to the bedroom to wake Stuart.

'It is 8 o'clock Stuart, you're going to be late.'

Stuart just groaned and turned over. 'Right,' he grunted.

'I've decided I am going to get a part time job now Ailsa is at school. It seems sensible to have some more money coming in.' Ann held her breath and waited for his response. It was best to just say it and get it over with. She was ready to leave the house straight away and take Ailsa to school if he reacted badly.

'Did you hear me, Stu?'

'I heard you, yes, do what you want if having a job makes you happy.'

Ann was relieved as she turned from the bedroom door towards the stairs. She felt more positive than she had in a while. At last, she was doing something for herself. She was glad she had made the decision to *tell* Stuart what she was doing, rather than asking permission. Picking her time wisely had been important to the outcome; she wagered that to mention it in passing when he was feeling tired and hung-over was the pathway to least resistance. It was also of no great surprise to her that he didn't complain. He knew that they were behind on the rent and if she was earning it would give him more money to spend on his precious beer. Now all she had to do was find work that would fit around school times.

CHAPTER 13

Carol

Ripon
1976

CAROL WAS EXCITED about looking round the two primary schools in Ripon. It was important that Sophie was settled and happy where she went to school and the friend's she made were important. It would be nice for Carol to meet some new friends too; she felt like she was outgrowing the mums she had met at the local mother and toddler's group in the church hall. They had been in their new home for over twelve months now and Carol had made a few friends but there wasn't any particular person that she had gotten close to. The new house was wonderful and it was the first time in their marriage that they had had this much space. They only had a small area to the front but the back garden was quite large, with plenty of room for Sophie to run around in.

Bill had decided that a move would do them both good. He wanted a house to move into that did not need anything doing to it. Their last home was lovely and had original sash windows and some period features but anything that needed doing always turned out to be a big job. Most of all, the new house had an en suite off the master bedroom. It was a new build and everything felt clean and fresh. They were even able to choose the colour it was painted. Life felt good right now. Bill was not working away for weeks on end anymore; he was based at the head office in Leeds and travelled in each day by car but was always home each evening. It was about time. When Carol looked back, she had been very resentful that once she had finally got home, and there seemed to be no lasting effects from the coma, he couldn't wait to get back on the oil rigs.

The only blot on the landscape now, was that, despite trying for the last couple of years for a second child, Carol had been unable to conceive. The doctors kept on telling them that there didn't appear to be any particular reason why this was the case but it just hadn't happened. With the inability to get pregnant, Carol had become quite low. The doctor had offered her antidepressants but Carol was not comfortable with taking the pills, and in any case, she had been there before and managed to get through without them. She'd had dark moods before.

There had been times, following the accident, when she just hadn't felt the same bond with her baby as she had before. She blamed this unusual lack of feelings on the fact that she had missed out on vital months with her child. It was as if Sophie wasn't part of her anymore. She had felt almost redundant and a little lost. Sophie had gotten used to Bill and Valerie, their neighbour before the move, who had helped them out whilst she had been in hospital. Nothing was too much trouble for Val; she devoted herself to supporting Bill when Carol had been absent. Carol felt rather ungrateful looking back. She was slightly ashamed at how resentful she'd felt towards her. She had been jealous of the way Sophie seemed calmer and happier when Val was around. It was only since moving, that Carol really felt like she had her daughter to herself and her confidence in her abilities as a mother fully started to take shape. She'd got through that and she would get through this.

'Come on, Sophie. Let's get your coat on; it's chilly out there. Do you remember that we are going to visit your new school?' Carol helped her daughter into a little blue woollen coat. It was a freezing November day but it was optimistically sunny and there was no sign of rain clouds.

'Yippee! new school!'

'You are not staying today. We are just visiting, alright,' Carol warned.

'Alright,' Sophie said, acceptingly.

The visit to the nursery would be for an hour, with the mums allowed to stay. Then, if Sophie was accepted and Carol liked the feel of the school, Sophie could start after Christmas. Five mornings a week to start, before going up to the reception class the following September. This was the school that Carol preferred but she had an appointment with the other school, St Johns, the following day, just to make sure. The next day she would leave Sophie with her friend, Kath, at the toddler group. There was no point in confusing Sophie at this stage by taking her along, not until Carol had made her mind up herself.

Baxter Street Primary was only a ten minute walk from their home and Carol arrived in good time with Sophie. There was a small entrance area, outside of the building, that housed the nursery class; it was already filling up with other mums and their children. All the mothers were smiling and chatting away, whilst the children eyed each other cautiously, some from behind the legs of their mothers. The smell of plasticine, glue and other familiar smells, took Carol back to her own childhood. Some smells never changed. A short, very round lady, wearing equally round rimmed glasses, threw open the door to the classroom with gusto.

'Goodness, what have we here then, lots of new boys and girls that want to come and play with myself and Miss Johnson.' The smiley teacher then crouched down and asked a little girl at the front, 'would you like to come and see the Wendy house?' And to a little boy standing next to her, 'and would you like to come and play with some cars in the sand pit?' No answer was required, as she then stood up and announced, 'my name is Mrs Drew and I may be your new teacher, along with Miss Johnson here. Now mums, if you would like to all come in and collect a name badge for yourself and your child from Miss Johnson, we can start to get to know one another.'

Everybody filed in, collecting their sticky label and being ushered here and there by the excitable Mrs Drew. It was clear that she had done this many times before and the children were soon going from area to area, dragging the hands of their mums to follow.

Sophie was extremely taken with the Wendy house and was soon chattering away to another little girl who was equally as chatty. Carol smiled as she saw them both grab a hand each of a small boy and pull him through the door.

'Looks like our girls are going to take charge of the men in their lives doesn't it?'

Carol turned her attention to the woman speaking to her. 'It certainly does look that way,' Carol replied.

The woman talking to her was a good foot taller than Carol and had short spiky blond hair. Her large round eyes had an elfin quality that matched her petite nose. 'My name is Olivia,' she said, gesturing to herself, 'and that's Vicki.' Her broad smiling mouth was out of proportion to her face and should have looked at odds with her other features but it worked perfectly and made her quite a stunning looking woman. She was wearing a faux fur jacket, which was well worn, and faded jeans with a multi-coloured scarf wrapped several times around her neck. The complete opposite to the way Carol herself was dressed.

'Hi, I'm Carol and that other bossy miss is Sophie. Pleased to meet you.'

'What are you thinking so far? I'm rather impressed up to now. The teachers seem quite fun and relaxed, which is good if they have to care for Vicki a few mornings each week. She can be quite a handful, or maybe it's that I'm not quite as good at being a mum as I should be. I think sometimes I laugh at her too much and then when I get cross at her for something naughty, I laugh as well. I'm not quite sure that is the way to do it. I find her totally draining some days.'

The woman called Olivia laughed at her last statement about finding her child totally draining, as if she found being drained by her child something funny. She hardly paused to take breath. It was as though she had to get all her information out within as short a space of time as possible.

'I think they are just at that age where they are full of questions and get bored with our answers. They are ready for new experiences, new friends, and new boundaries to push,' Carol said. She could not believe the whole boundary statement she had just made. Even to herself, it sounded like a quote from one of those well-meaning books and she felt slightly awkward. 'What I mean, is that they like to try our patience. They watch for our reactions to certain behaviour. It is time for them to try pushing those boundaries with new people,' she paused, realising what she had just said and blushed slightly. 'Goodness that came over as patronising, didn't it? I am sure you are doing just fine! They can all be a handful from time to time,' she added. Carol felt very clumsy with how she had responded but Olivia just beamed at her.

'Absolutely. Couldn't have put it any better myself actually, not at all patronising. I asked the question. It's like she behaves with me one way and her father another and her granny differently again. Vicki gets away with all sorts with me, and her father tells me I am too soft, but then he is soft in ways that I'm not and her granny thinks she wraps us both around her little finger. Nursery should give her some basic rules which we can try and impose at home. Well, hopefully - that's the idea at least. It is hard to get cross with them don't you think?' she looked across the room, to where their children were playing, 'they are just so cute and funny most of the time.' Olivia beamed and laughed again.

Carol immediately warmed to this happy and optimistic woman, who found everything so funny.

'I think this nursery is lovely and the teachers seem ever so nice. Have you looked around St John's yet? I have an appointment tomorrow.'

'Gosh, yes I did. Last week. Heard terrific things about them but I wasn't that keen myself. I was introduced to the nursery teacher, Mrs Summers, very briefly by the school secretary, a mouse of a woman, who timidly knocked on the Nursery door and asked if it was possible for me to have a quick look around. As I didn't have an appointment, I was told that it would interfere with the children's routine to take me in to look around. I had a peep through the window. The facilities looked fine, but I found Mrs Summers very scary. There was nothing 'summer' like about her demeanour in the slightest, more 'Mrs Winter' if you ask me, and she had frightful whiskers protruding, not only form her top lip and chin, but poking out of her nose! It was awful. I couldn't look her in the eye when she spoke to me; I was fixated on a particularly long hair on her chin that must have been at least two inches in length.' Olivia's voice had dropped to an inconspicuous tone as she spoke and moved closer to be heard only by Carol. Suddenly, moving away and raising her voice again, she continued, 'Of course, you must make up your own mind. But quite honestly, I just had visions of being called in to the school on Vicki's first day and being asked to remove her for telling Mrs Summers that she could borrow her daddy's razor if hers had broken because she needed a shave!'

Carol could not contain her laughter and that set Olivia off into a fit of giggles. They were like a pair of schoolgirls. They both had tears running down their faces.

When they had got themselves together, Carol said, 'How am I ever going to get through my appointment without falling about laughing. I just can't go now.'

Olivia grinned at her.

'Oh, you should go, even just to put your mind at rest that you have made the right choice… or if you've never seen a bearded lady close up before.'

They both started giggling again.

'Hmm. I'll think about it but this place is looking better to me by the minute.'

The two women spoke briefly to a couple of the other mothers but mostly chatted with each other whilst watching Sophie and Vicki drag a boy, whom they had learned was called Christopher, around by the hand from activity to activity. The hour went quickly. Soon, Mrs Drew announced it was tidy up time. Mrs Drew explained to the children that when 'tidy up time' was announced, they each had to pick up two play toys from the area and put them in the tidy away basket, which she held up to demonstrate. The children happily did as they were asked.

'I am definitely transferring that idea to home. Look at Vicki: she can't get enough toys in her arms. She has at least three!'

Carol agreed.

'Yes, definitely a good idea. Make it second nature, whilst they still think it's fun.'

All the children said their goodbyes and filed to the coat pegs, near the door, to get their hats and coats on. The poor boy named Christopher had to be prised out of the clutches of the two little girls who were reluctant to let him go. As each parent left, they were given a letter with the date for the new intake and a form to sign and fill in to request a place for the January term. The mums and children said their goodbyes and Carol and Olivia parted company just outside the playground gates.

'Well then, Sophie, did you enjoy nursery school?'

'It was great,' Sophie replied, excitedly. 'Can I go and see Vicki there again tomorrow, Mummy?'

'Not tomorrow sweetheart. It will be after Christmas when you go again. Remember I told you that was just a visit to see if you liked it?'

'I liked Vicki. She was funny. I want to play with her again tomorrow.'

'Well I'm sorry sweetheart but you may have to wait.'

'Don't want to wait. We can go to her house and we can play there.'

'Sorry honey but I don't know where she lives. I didn't ask her mummy.'

'Why not?'

'I just didn't think to.'

'Why not?'

'Because I just didn't.'

'Oh, well can you telephone her mummy and ask where her house is?'

'No, sweetheart, because I don't know her telephone number. I'm sorry.'

'Why not?'

'Because I didn't ask her mummy.'

'Oh,' Sophie said, thoughtfully. 'You are a silly Mummy!'

Carol laughed and bent down to tickle her daughter, 'I am a silly mummy, sometimes, but I am good at tickling!'

Carol felt very content on their walk home. She had enjoyed her morning and her mind was more or less made up. This nursery was the right one for Sophie and the fact that she had already made a friend, was a positive step. Carol was sure she had also made a new friend in Olivia. Perhaps she really was turning a corner. There had been no black moods in nearly six months now, so perhaps when Sophie was settled into nursery after Christmas, she would think about getting a couple of mornings a week doing some office or shop work. They didn't need the money but it may be good for her to find an interest outside of the house. Carol would chat with Bill later and see what he thought. Bill would encourage her, she was positive, as he worried that she spent too much time in her own company.

They were soon back home walking up the driveway to the front door of Carol's new home. She was looking forward to some soup to warm them up on the chilly day. It's funny, Carol thought, how things can seem so bleak some days and brighter on others, for no real reason.

CHAPTER 14

Carol

Ripon
1977
Queen's Jubilee Party

'THE ROAD LOOKS absolutely amazing!' Bill had told her for the third time that day, 'why don't you just try to get up and get dressed for Sophie's sake and come to the street party this afternoon?' He moved over to the window to draw back the curtains, 'we won't get another Queen's Jubilee Street party to celebrate again. We are making history here, Carol. Olivia has called you several times and quite frankly it is getting embarrassing having to make excuses.'

'Nobody asked you to make excuses. Why can't you just understand it? I cannot face people, noise or anything when I feel like this. It's not like I want to be difficult. I just cannot face it. I have no energy.'

'Alright honey,' he reluctantly closed the curtains again, 'I won't press you to do something you are not up to but if you change your mind, we will only be outside,' he moved back towards the door, 'perhaps if you sleep a bit longer you will feel up to coming down in a while.' Bill left his wife in bed, with the room in darkness, and went downstairs to where his daughter was playing.

'Well tiger, it's just me and you today for the party. Mummy still has a headache. Is that ok?'

'Daddy, you are silly. Have you forgotten that Vicki is coming to play as well and Liv?'

'No. I haven't forgotten they're coming but I had better let Vicki's mummy know that your mummy is not well.'

'Daddy, me and Vicki can still play can't we? pleeaase?'

'I will just check with Vicki's mummy now.'

Sophie went back to playing with her dolls and Bill called Olivia.

'Hi Grahame – it's Bill.'

'Hi mate. You ok?'

'I am, thanks. But Carol has one of her heads and is not up to the street party. Are you guys still up for coming? Sophie will never forgive us if she doesn't get to play with Vicki. She's been really looking forward to it.'

'Sure, don't see why not. I'll put Liv on.'

'Hi Bill. Carol still not good?'

'No, afraid not, but I don't want to spoil things for the girls. You will all still come over to the party, won't you?'

'As if we would miss out on all those fancy hotdogs at the posh new end of town. I mean, oh my, as if you need to ask. The girls would absolutely go ape if we stopped them meeting today. It's all they've talked about all week. We'll be there, no fear. I take it Carol wasn't up for a chat?'

'No. I'm sorry Liv. I just don't know what to do. I'll talk to you guys in a bit. You know little ears and all that.'

'Sure, no worries Bill. We'll bring some beers and I've done a large batch of fairy cakes, more than enough for both our contributions, so don't worry.'

'Thanks Liv. You're a star; she sure fell lucky when you two met and became friends.'

'We both did. Try to be patient Bill. I'm sure it's difficult. Carol doesn't want to feel like this. It's just that anxiety and depression are so hard to treat and, yeah, I know you've heard it a thousand times. Anyway, just make sure you have plenty of cider when we arrive!'

'Sure have! I will see you guys in a while, bye.'

'Bye Bill - chin up.'

Bill put down the phone.

Bill could never have imagined Liv getting depressed; she was always so upbeat but she and Carol had become close in just a few months and Liv got Carol. It was a relief to Bill that at last there was somebody he could talk to that seemed to understand. He hated to admit it but Carol had lost touch with what few friends they had had the last few years and he could see it happening again. It wasn't something he could point out easily, as it was part of the problem. Carol would just get low and cancel arrangements or not make the effort like she used to before Sophie was born. Some friends just stopped calling and he couldn't blame them. It hurt him, though, to see this. He loved her so damn much. The bloody crash had started it all off but he just didn't know how to make it go away.

'They're coming Tiger!' Bill turned to his daughter, who was tucking her doll into her doll's pram like a true professional.

'Yay! I can't wait to see Vicki. We are taking our babies to the party with us.'

'That's a lovely idea, tiger.'

'Is Vicki nearly here?'

'Not quite, but not long. Let's go and get you dressed into your party dress, shall we?'

'The one with the red flowers on, Daddy - I like that one. Can I wear my party shoes too?'

'Yes, the one with the red flowers on and your party shoes.'

'Who is going to do my hair if Mummy is poorly? You are no good at plaits, Daddy.'

'Well, princess, I thought we could ask Liv when she gets here. I'm sure she can do plaits as she is a mummy too.'

His daughter put her forefinger to her lip and cocked her head to one side in a thoughtful manner, as she had seen her teacher do at school; it was what Mrs Drew did when she was trying to show the children that she was giving a matter some extra special thought.

'I suppose that will be alright; she does make plaits in Vicki's hair sometimes.'

Bill took his daughter by her still, baby-like, chubby hand and led her upstairs to get her changed for the party.

Sophie was still fussing over her doll, having changed its clothes at least several times, when he heard the doorbell chime. He himself had changed into some light-weight beige slacks and a white T-Shirt. It was promising to be a scorcher of a day.

'Hi guys, come on in. Hey there Vicki, you are looking rather pretty. Is that your party dress?'

'No, it's a sundress but it's a pretty sundress, especially for parties.'

Vicki ran off into the front lounge to find Sophie.

'Phew,' said Liv, as she followed her husband in with bags in either hand, 'that was a close call. The only real party dress she has is longed sleeved crushed velvet, which is far too warm for outside today. I had a right fight to get her to put on something more suitable. It took us twenty minutes with all of her dresses on and off several times before we convinced her that the one she is now wearing, was a sundress fancy enough to be suitable for this infernal street party. I thought we would never get here.'

Grahame had been standing there, quietly letting his wife vent. He was a nice chap but a little on the quiet side. Bill and he hit it off quite well. He may be quiet, which was not surprising because Liv talked enough for the pair of them, but he had a wicked dry sense of humour.

'Hmm, I wonder where she gets that from. How many times was it this morning that you changed outfits?'

'Grahame, that really is not the same thing at all. I had to change because I couldn't find a dress that would fit me. I really cannot understand why they felt so tight; I didn't think that I had gained that much weight since last year. It was really a matter of which dress I could feel comfortable in.'

Grahame just raised his eyebrows but made no comment.

'Now, Bill, the cakes are in a Tupperware box in this bag and I've made a pile of sandwiches, they just need plating up and putting on the trestle table that we are eating at. There are also some drinks in this bag. Perhaps I can trust you boys with putting them in the correct place and watching the girls whilst I pop up and have a quick check on Carol?' With that, she thrust both bags into Bill's hands and practically ran up the stairs before either man could reply, shouting, 'marvellous! Smashing! Leave you to it then,' as she went.

Carol and Bill's bedroom was the second room on the right off the landing and the door was shut. Liv knocked gently on the door and went in without waiting for a reply. The room was near pitch black, so Liv went to the window and pulled the curtains apart slightly so she could see her friend. Carol turned over and pushed herself up slightly into a sitting position.

'Hey, you. It's gorgeous out there. It's the most fabulous day for a street party. Why didn't you call me back?'

'I'm sorry, Liv. I told Bill to tell you; I just have felt so rubbish, head pounding and no energy. I couldn't face talking.'

'Yes, I got the usual excuses from Bill. Bless him, Carol, he really is so worried about you. We both are.'

Carol just shrugged her shoulders.

'You have to fight this thing. Whatever it is that gets you so down. It has to be tackled.'

'What? Pumped full of pills? That doesn't really help. I just need to sleep. I just get these reoccurring nightmares. They leave me so exhausted and anxious for days. The doctor just wants to give me sleeping pills and anti-depressants. They really are not the answer.'

'Well what do you think the answer is?'

'I don't know, Liv. I know I should try and do something but I feel so trapped by these feelings of fear. I'm not even sure what I'm frightened of.'

'You told me that before having Sophie, you were fine. Do you think it is some sort of post-natal depression that you have never gotten over, or do you think it was that train crash you were involved in?'

'Honestly, I think it has to do with the crash and not being able to look after Sophie properly by myself following the accident. I can't even remember fully what happened that day. I have had to piece it together from what everyone else has told me. Except the nightmares bring back the most awful images and feelings and it's like I'm missing something but I don't know what. I'm not even sure if I want to remember. It's just the most ghastly feeling. Do you know that I haven't even met up with my friend Jenny since it all happened because it frightens me? She was part of that awful day. I don't want to go back to that place. We used to be so close and I have made excuse after excuse each time she has suggested we meet up, it's pathetic. Now, she doesn't even try to arrange anything.'

Liv sat and listened to her friend thoughtfully.

'Well, maybe that is a good place to start. Face the fear. It cannot be any worse than what you are feeling right now and in fact, it just might help. Call her and arrange to meet. Go on the train. Take the journey. Ask her about the day. Go back to the last memory you had when you set off that morning and try and piece it together. Whatever she can tell you may in turn help you to remember.'

'God, I haven't even been on a train since it happened! The thought terrifies me.'

'The thought of it terrifies you, but actually doing it may not be as terrifying as you imagine. You won't know until you try.'

'Oh, I'm not sure Liv, and even if I did, how can that help with how I'm feeling? I mean really?'

'I have no idea but I read a book recently, written by some big wig in psychology, who said that the thought of what you are afraid of is worse than facing it head on. In any case it's worth a try, don't you think? The worst case scenario is that you will catch up with an old dear friend. I call that win, win in my book. Now stop moping, get dressed, and get some sunshine on your face. Everything looks better in the sun. Do you know some days, when I'm blue, I take the shade off my table lamp and get as close to it as I can with my eyes closed and pretend that it's sunny? I swear it helps. The only thing is that one day I got too close and burnt the end of my nose and had to walk around with a big blister on the end of it for a few days. It was awfully embarrassing - the looks that I got! Grahame thought I was losing the plot. That was in the early days. He is quite used to me now. Either that, or he just pretends not to be shocked at some of the things that I do. He wasn't pleased last week though. He came home from work to find a massive vase of flowers in the dining room. At first, he admired them and said they were lovely, until he saw the card next to them.'

'Why? Who were they from?'

'They were from me, to me. I bought them at the new florist in the village. I couldn't resist. When I was paying for them, the lady asked if I wanted a card to go with them, so I took it and wrote it out when I got home.'

'Alright,' said Carol, with a grin on her face, 'what did you write?' Carol found herself laughing at her friend, despite how she was feeling.

It said, 'To Liv, you have worked really hard this week and you have done a fantastic job. Please accept these flowers and enjoy them, as you really deserve them.'

'Oh Liv! You didn't? Were they expensive? Did Grahame go mad?'

'Yes! And yes! But I did deserve them. They still look lovely and they have made me happy. I deserve to be happy and once his blood pressure had returned to normal, I'm sure Grahame thought I deserved them too.

Anyway, it doesn't matter really. I decided that it was high time that I had flowers and I wanted them, so that is that, as far as I am concerned.'

Carol couldn't help but admire Liv's enthusiastic approach to life. Nothing seemed to grind her down and if it did, she always found a way to deal with it in her own unique way. Perhaps she would give the matter of meeting up with Jenny some thought and maybe an hour at the street party may help a little bit.

'Come on, come on, up and face the day. All the little cakes are made and sandwiches too. The boys are taking charge of setting things out at our table. We can wait for you to get dressed.'

'I look a fright and my hair needs washing. I'm not sure.'

'Well, wash it. Jump in the shower. It will soon dry out there. I'll tell you what, I will go check on the boys and girls and come back in about half an hour. I'm not taking no for an answer.' With that, Liv leapt off the bed and was out of the door before Carol could protest any further. 'Girls, girls come on are you ready?' Liv shouted, as she descended the stairs.

'Mummy, you forgot to bring my pram for Annabelle!' Vicki was stood at the door of the lounge with her arms crossed and an angry expression on her face.

'Well, then how about Annabelle shares Lilly-Rae's pram?'

'Sophie said there's not enough room!'

'Oh, I'm sure there is.' Liv escorted her grumpy daughter into the lounge where Sophie was stood protectively over her doll's pram, 'Sophie, what do you say the babies share the pram like sisters?'

'No room!'

'Well, how about we take out teddy and make room for Annabelle? Then, your babies can be like sisters and both enjoy the party and chat to each other.'

Sophie did her thoughtful pose again, tilting her head to one side.

'Sisters? Alright, that's a good idea! And me and Vicki can be sisters taking our babies to the party!' She declared, excitedly.

'Yes!' Shouted Vicki, 'we can be sisters too!'

Sophie turned to Liv, 'as we're sisters, can you do my hair like Vicki's? Daddy said you could probably do plaits but I want my hair in a bun like Vicki.'

'That's a good idea,' chirped Vicki, 'then we will look like proper sisters.'

'O.K,' said Sophie, 'I'm the big sister though, because it's my pram, and you haven't to be bossy as I'm the eldest.'

'O.K and I will be very kind,' said Vicki, 'I'm always kind. Aren't I, Mummy?'

'Umm, well yes, Vicki, you certainly try to be most of the time.'

The day turned out to be hot. They had been so lucky with the weather. There was plenty of juice and drinks to keep everyone cool and hydrated. The street had bunting in red, white and blue, which was hung from lamppost to lamppost. Trestle tables had been lined up along the road and a good spread of food was laid out in Tupperware boxes and foil covered plates to stop it drying out in the sun. The tables were covered in white paper cloths with paper plates, streamers, and blowers for the children. The Bay City Rollers was played through loudspeakers, donated from one of the neighbours for use during the party. Along the pavement, were different stalls set up with things for the children to take part in, which didn't cost anything. Everybody had helped and donated items for a food hamper. Each family that came was given a raffle ticket and everybody contributed food. The atmosphere was wonderful. All the neighbours were there. Some had brought along friends who were not having street parties themselves. Everyone wanted to celebrate the Queen's Jubilee. There were smiles all round. The happy chatter and laughter of children could be heard echoing around the neighbourhood. Each end of the street had been cordoned off and parents were taking it in turns to stand vigilantly at each end so none of the children could wander away. At about 4pm it was announced that the fancy hat parade would commence in 10 minutes and all the children should start to congregate at one end of the street so they could show off their creations and be judged. The girls put on their hats and assembled at the far end of the street. The doll's pram had been forgotten about for the moment. There were some spectacular entries and Carol did have to wonder how many of the children had really made their own hat or crown. Olivia and Carol, having made the basic hat, had encouraged the girls to do their own decorating, even though it had been a traumatic affair. They had to both help the process slightly by re-sticking items back on, so on the whole, it was their own design. They both looked extremely proud plodding around with cheesy grins on their faces and they got a cheer from their parents as they paraded past. This made them both smile and giggle, their hands firmly holding tight to one another. The winner was announced but all the children were congratulated on their efforts and awarded a tube of sweets as a reward for having taken part.

Although there were times in the day that Carol had struggled, she was pleased that she had made the effort. There were moments where she had felt a little disjointed from the things going on around her, only to be shaken out of her reverie by some comment Olivia had made. Her head still felt heavy with a dull ache at the back of her eyes. The main thing was that she had managed.

Carol snuggled down next to Bill later that night, feeling a little happier. He was already snoring gently next to her, fast asleep. He really had been so patient with her over the years; she was lucky to have him. Carol mulled over the conversation she had had with Olivia earlier today. The time had not been right earlier in the evening to talk to Bill about the possibility of meeting up with Jenny. It had turned into such a pleasant day and she hadn't wanted to bring it down. The excitement of the day started to vanish, as Carol's fear of another night's sleep being invaded by nightmares, started to creep into her thoughts. Lying there, she tried to push all thoughts of anything other than today's activities from her mind. She closed her eyes and pictured the girl's smiling faces. Bill and Grahame pulling each other's legs. Carol, surprisingly, slowly drifted into a dream free sleep.

CHAPTER 15

Ann

Cudibrook - Scotland
1977
Queen's Jubilee

A ILSA WAS STAYING the night with a school friend, so she was safe. Ann looked around the bedroom at the mess that had been made. Clothes were pulled from drawers and there was a glass ornament smashed and ground into the carpet. He knew that it was from her mum. It meant so much to her. He was standing in the bedroom doorway. She walked slowly over to him. His beefy arm, resting across the door frame, was stopping her from leaving.

'Can I pass, please?'

'Can you pass?' he sneers, enunciating each word slowly.

Spittle lands on her cheek. She can smell the stale smell of whiskey from his rank breath. He has started with the whiskey now. Not content with just beer. It probably started a while ago, she thought, randomly.

She knows what's coming as she stands in front of him. She doesn't look at him. She closes her eyes.

'You're going nowhere,' he screamed in her face. His forehead touched hers.

She waits. The silence stretches between them and then it comes.

'Bitch!'

Everything went black.

PART 2

CHAPTER 16

Sophie

Manchester
Aug 1996

S OPHIE HAD SPENT most of the morning going through file after file. The temp they employed to work in their department for two weeks had caused considerable chaos. Sophie had drawn the short straw in having to sort out all the mistakes she had left behind. No wonder the temp, Melisa, had seemed so efficient. Now she knew how she had managed to get through her work so quickly. Document after document had been literally stuffed into files. Important documents had not been sent out and some documents were in completely the wrong files. A rather abusive telephone call the previous day had ended up coming through to Sophie's phone. Joseph Prichard, of Davies and Davies, had told her he thought they were incompetent idiots for failing to send out the draft contract to their firm and had resulted in a delay in completion of a property sale. This meant his client wouldn't get the keys to their new property for the agreed completion date. They were right, of course; it was incompetent. It was, however, not her personal incompetence. Sophie was meticulous with her case files and had an excellent work ethic. It really cheesed her off that temps like Melisa gave firms a bad name. They 'swanned' in and got paid, probably more pro-rata than she did, and then she had to sort their mess out.

'Want a cup of my lovely tea to cheer you up, sweet cheeks?'

Sophie looked up from the file she was working on, to see Stevie, her friend and colleague, leaning on her desk. Sophie couldn't help but smile. Stevie was one damn good breath of 'camp' fresh air. Even his business suit, with overly tight trousers and fitted jacket, accentuated the fact that he was out and proud.

'That would be lovely, Stevie. You're a star.'

'I know! So Jason tells me every day.'

Jason was Stevie's partner of fourteen years. They were madly in love and didn't care who knew it.

'So, how's it going? Many more cock ups to sort? You'd think this place would have learnt by now - that temp agency they use is absolutely useless. Listen sweetie, don't take it to heart what that silly toss pot Prichard said. He knows these things happen. He's all hot air. He obviously didn't get any this weekend. His firm did the same thing to us last month with one of our clients. He is probably just pissed because he plays golf with that big wig client. It is a known fact that he is such a sycophant with him. It was bound to make him blow a gasket if anything went wrong. I could personally wring that Melisa's scrawny little neck myself.'

Sophie knew Stevie was right. They had known Jones, said client, was a close friend of Prichard's. Prichard had made it clear in a conversation a few weeks earlier, when they had taken the case on. Sophie would never normally have let a temp near any case she had opened but she had been called away last week. Her mum had another of her 'episodes'. It was partly her fault, as she should have made sure that she had passed the file to Stevie before she had left. It was just that she didn't think she would have been gone for more than a couple of days.

'Right. Well, there is no point in moaning. I just need to finish this lot and put it behind me. Fancy lunch in The Farrier? I feel like being a pig and having their homemade steak pie with chips. Comfort food is what I crave right now.'

'You bet your sweet ass, darling. Although I am more fancying a large glass of red myself - hair of the, proverbial, dog and all that. Jason did us a romantic candlelit dinner last night as he wanted to celebrate. He has landed another job with a bistro in Cheshire. They want designs for a full refurb. Let's just say that one bottle turned into two. I will leave the rest to your imagination.'

'You two are terrible. I don't know how you do it and still come in looking so good.'

'Practice darling. A lot of practice.'

Sophie laughed as he flounced away, swinging his hips across the office to his own desk. He gave her a cheeky little wink as he sat down and picked up his phone to make a call.

The rest of the morning went very quickly, with no more dramas. They were soon seated in the Farrier with a large glass of red in front of them.

'I feel very decadent, not to mention a little guilty, getting a large glass of wine as well as a big plate of pie and chips. Still, it is just what I needed.'

'Sweet cheeks, you need to do it more often. You take life far too seriously. You're twenty- five, not forty- five for God's sake. Stop being so perfect and sensible.'

'I know, I know, so you tell me every other week. I am what I am, Stevie. I do try to be more fun but some of us just don't have your grand outlook on life. It takes more effort for some of us.'

'Well, I have an idea to give you some down time and chill out for a while. So, hear me out before you go all practical on me. I thought we could have a few days away at that boarding house your mad grandmother runs. I know she drives you mad but she is good fun by the sounds of it and I am dying to meet her. Jason needs to go away on business next week, so you and I can take Devon by storm. We are both owed plenty of days holiday, so we should just be spontaneous and do it.'

'Oh, I don't know, Stevie. I've only just got back from being off for a few days, also I'm not sure it's your sort of place and it is not a boarding house, thank you. My granny would go mad if she heard you refer to it as that. It's very upmarket didn't you know.'

'Well hush my mouth! B&B then, hotel, whatever. Everywhere is my sort of place, sweet cheeks. You need a break. You are owed the days in holidays, so why not. All this business with your mother is taking its toll. You need a bit of fun, excitement, thrills, etcetera, etcetera. I have awards in all of them.'

'Well, it does sound tempting. Do you think Jason will be alright with us going away together?'

'Darling, as much as I love you, I cannot be turned. It was his idea, if you must know. He suggested we have a few days away together because I was moaning that he is always away having fun without me. He thinks you keep me on the straight and narrow for some unfathomable reason.' Stevie gave her that butter wouldn't melt in his mouth look but with his pouty lip.

'I'm not sure anyone can keep you on the straight and narrow but I do my best. You shouldn't be so mean to Jason either; it is work that takes him away. He isn't on a jolly. It would be a nice idea but don't expect too much in the way of partying. It's not that sort of place.'

'That's fine by me girlfriend. I need to take in the more relaxing aspects of life. If it gets too boring, I'm sure we can liven things up a bit.'

'Oh lord, that's what I mean, don't be leading my Gran astray,' she laughed, 'she is bad enough as it is. I swear she doesn't realise she's in her seventies, not seventeen.'

'Sweet cheeks, you are so straight. There's nothing wrong with that. See, comments like that, is why you need to loosen up a little. A break with me and Grandmamma is just what you need.'

They finished their lunch and went back to the office. Sophie felt a little light-headed from the wine at lunch. She was most definitely a light weight but she knew a few days away with Stevie would do her the world of good. Perhaps she should call her grandmother tonight.

Sophie had been worrying about her mum more than usual, lately. Carol, her mum, had suffered with occasional bouts of depression for as long as Sophie could remember. Dad had said that it hadn't always been this way; there had been some sort of accident when Sophie was a baby. Her mum and Sophie had survived when others had died. Her dad had told her that her mum had struggled, on and off, since then with mood swings. They had never discussed it in front of Sophie, so she knew little about the details.

Lately, her mum had been struck down by severe headaches, which the G.P had said was due to stress. The daft thing was that her mum didn't have stress, so Sophie could not understand why the G.P had made this diagnosis.

Mum had tried to hide things from her, so that whenever Sophie tried to talk to her about the moods and headaches, she would just smile and tell her not to worry. In all other areas they were quite open with one another. Sophie could tell her anything and she never passed judgement. If she didn't approve, she may point out her misgivings but never pushed the matter. Eventually, Sophie would figure stuff out herself. Most of her friends said she was a cool mum. Her house was the one they all hung out at when they were all teenagers. Her mother had been adamant that she wasn't allowed to walk around the streets or hang around the park, like many of her friends did. However, she was the only one whose mother had welcomed a large group to congregate at their house. Her mum kept out of the way, in another room, whilst they had their teenage gossips. She smiled at the memory of hordes of kids piling into the house each night, her parents, suffering through the noise. Poor Dad, they even took over the television most weekends.

Sophie's mind turned to her gran. It had been at least a year since she had last seen her and she knew that Grandma Jane would be thrilled to see her - of that, she had no doubt. She would welcome Stevie like a long lost son. Her gran was lovely like that; she had always welcomed Sophie's friends. She was a little on the eccentric side and most certainly a little bit 'lady of the manor', without the money, but ever so nice. Sophie loved her to pieces but her mother and gran were quite distant. Sophie's mum had always maintained that her gran was a rather cold fish. Sophie couldn't understand why her mother felt this, especially when she herself got along famously with her. Grandma Jane was not the hugging type but she did go through the motions. There was a childlike exuberance in her attitude to life.

Her grandfather Joe was very down to earth. Jane was the lady of her manor and Joe was like the gardener, come odd job man. They made for a great and rather fun combination as a couple. Joe was her mother's stepfather but, to Sophie, had always been 'Gramps'.

That evening, in her small bedsit, Sophie snuggled down into the sofa, her comfort nest she called it. Having had a hot shower and made her-self a milky drink, she dialled her gran's number.

'Good evening, Sand Banks. How may I help you?'

Her granny had her best telephone voice on, it made Sophie smile.

"Granny, it's Sophie.'

'Sophie, darling thing, how are you?'

'Good thanks Granny, and how are things with you and Gramps?'

'You know us, darling. We are still moving, breathing and have a pulse, so all is good in the world.' Her gran gave a little laugh as she delivered her reply.

'Well, that is always good to hear. How is the business doing?'

'Slow to start with this season but picking up a bit. When are you going to visit? You are very overdue coming to see us, young lady. We have both missed you terribly.'

'That's why I'm calling. I have a friend who wants to have a break away and we thought it would be lovely to take in some sea air, plus he's dying to meet you and Gramps.'

'Well now, a *he* you say. That sounds most intriguing. Is it a special someone, may I pry?'

'Sorry to disappoint, Granny, but no! He sort of doesn't do girls.'

'Goodness, doesn't do girls? How very thrilling and most liberating of you to have puff as a friend, dear.'

'Granny! Don't call him that, for goodness sake. The term is gay. You are naughty still using that word these days. I'm sure you will love him - he is a lot of fun.'

'You know your Gramps and I are very modern with our outlook. All this politically correct stuff is so confusing darling, I meant no offence. We are not at all bothered what people are. We say live and let live. Will you want to share a room? I'm not quite sure how these things work.'

'Granny, it is not confusing. I think you just say those things to shock me. Please don't do that in front of Stevie though, I would hate him to be offended. It would be better to have separate rooms, if you can manage that, and we will pay for our rooms. You are running a business after all.'

'I promise to behave myself and you most certainly will not be paying to come and visit your grandparents. When were you thinking of coming?'

Sophie laughed. 'Early next Saturday morning. We thought we would stay until mid- week, which will give us around 5 days to chill out.'

'That is splendid and absolutely no problem. We have three rooms spare over the next three weeks. It will be good to have some young company. We only have a few oldies in right now and we are, quite frankly, sick of listening to them drone on about their aches and pains. Your grandfather will be so excited when I tell him you are coming. Talking of aches and pains, how is your mother this week? Your father told me she has been getting more of her heads and has been down in the dumps again the last few weeks?'

'A bit better. It's just more of the same Granny. As soon as she stops taking her tablets she seems to go back into her depression. I wish she would just stay on them. She was in quite a dark place last week. Dad has asked her to go back to the doctors about the headaches, or, to at least talk to them about how she is feeling, but you know mum, she won't always do what is best for her.'

'Your mother has always had a mind of her own. I have tried to tell her not to stop taking them just because she feels better but she doesn't listen. Her head always gets worse when she comes off her medication.'

'I know, Granny. It's difficult but we just have to be patient.'

Sophie did not want to get too deep into this one. Her gran and mother would never see eye to eye. It was such a shame. Sophie had tried on numerous occasions to bridge the gap, only to realise that it was just never going to happen. After Sophie ended her call with her gran, she called Stevie to let him know the trip was on.

CHAPTER 17

Sophie

Manchester
Aug 1996

THE FOLLOWING SATURDAY morning they set off. It was looking like a rather miserable day for August. Sophie was doing the driving down to Devon, as Stevie was not a morning person. When she pulled up outside his flat at about 5.30 am, she was amazed to see him trundle out of the foyer with his small weekend case on wheels. Sophie was most surprised, if not impressed.

'Good lord! I thought I would have to drag you out of bed. Look at you, all ready and raring to go!'

'It wasn't through choice,' Stevie grumped. 'Bloody Jason had a 7.30am flight and he brought us breakfast in bed. Why would anyone want to eat at such an ungodly hour?'

'Oh, I think that is so sweet and romantic. You should be pleased he cares so much to make the effort.'

'Don't be fooled, darling - he was after morning delights...'

'Oh, Stevie. Really, do you have to?'

'No, darling, I don't and I didn't. Comprende!'

They both were in fits of laughter.

'You are such a breath of fresh air. What would I do without you?'

'I don't know but, right now, I need some shut eye, so you will jolly well have to do without me for a while. I have at least two hours sleep to catch up on. Wake me when you want a break from driving.'

Sophie didn't mind driving. In fact, she enjoyed it. When it was early like this, it was the best time of the day. The air always smelt fresher, sweeter somehow, before the traffic built up and started to pollute the air. The day may have started off a bit miserable but you never knew, it could turn out to be glorious. She felt happier today than she had felt in a while. As the miles sped by, she felt herself starting to really unwind and relax and look forward to seeing the beautiful Devon countryside once again.

Sand Banks Bed and Breakfast was on the South Devonshire Coast. It sat in a bay, on the coastland. It was about 2 miles to the nearest village of Ashburton and was set in the most beautiful surroundings. Large gardens, only partly kept in check, enclosed the fourteen-bed roomed Victorian house. The views from the bedrooms, at the back of the house, were breath-taking. It took in the bay, which shelved gently down over sand dunes, to the sea. The beach itself could be reached by a small path and steps that started at the end of the gardens, which Sand Banks was nestled in. The lovely thing about this house was that it was so quiet and private. It had been described by many of its regular visitors as a hidden oasis of tranquillity and charm. Her gran and Joe had been lucky. When they had bought it, well over thirty years ago, it had been rather neglected and unloved. They purchased it at a good price and had taken out a small loan to do immediate repairs. It had been their dream. Between them, they had turned the place into quite a lovely bed and breakfast. They could have called it a hotel, had they offered more than breakfast, but had decided that that would mean having to take on more staff and a lot of extra work. Jane and Joe were both in agreement - staff were a headache. Guests were one thing. Staff was another thing, entirely. They seemed to manage very well with a couple of part time ladies from the village and a young man that sorted the breakfasts out, as well as helping to maintain the large gardens. Even those they employed now had only been there the last couple of years. Before that, they had done it all themselves.

Sophie pulled into a service station just as Stevie had started to come around. He straightened from his slumped position next to her in the car and rubbed his eyes, then stretched.

'How long have I been asleep, sweet cheeks?'

'Long enough. You were snoring like a drain. It's a wonder you didn't wake yourself up. We come off at the next junction and then it starts to get more pleasant. You have slept all through the boring bit of the drive.'

'How long until we arrive at the manor of *Lady Jane's*?'

'About an hour and a quarter,' Sophie laughed at Stevie's name for her grandmother.

'Oh my Lord. Have I been out that long?'

'You most certainly have. Don't worry, though; I'm used to the drive. To be honest I'm not sure I am happy about you driving my Phoebe anyway.'

'How very dare you! I am an excellent driver.'

'Save it for the person's brick wall you demolished last month, when you parked your car and forgot to apply the handbrake.'

'Oh, now come on, that's below the belt. You promised you wouldn't mention that again. It was bad enough apologising to the police for reporting it stolen when it disappeared from outside Sandra's house. Not to mention the humiliation, without my friends reminding me every chance they get,' he said, pouting.

Sandra was Stevie's sister. He'd been visiting her when the unfortunate car incident occurred. Sophie laughed so much on the Monday morning, when Stevie had told her what had happened, that she had been unable to get her breath. The sad fact was that most of the office had reacted in the same way. It wasn't the fact that the car had rolled into the brick wall, causing immense damage to both wall and car. It was the fact that when he couldn't see it parked outside his sister's house from the window, half an hour after he arrived, he had screamed in panic and reported it stolen to the police. At the same time the person whose garden wall it was in-bedded in had also reported an incident. Stevie, bless him, could not understand why they had thought it was so funny. His ego and pride had taken a bashing - much like the ill-fated vehicle.

'Sorry. It's too good a laugh to pass up. Come on, Stevie. Don't say you wouldn't mention it every chance you got if it was me.'

'Well, maybe I would but you're not as sensitive as me. Jason was so angry he made me cry. I am still very traumatized by the whole incident.

Not to mention I have to put up with Jason moaning on about his clean driving history and his bloody no claims bonus.'

'Ok, I'm sorry. Let's go and use the loo and grab a coffee. There are no loo stops now until we get to Grans.'

They were soon back inside the warmth of Sophie's car, clutching steaming coffee. It had been quite busy at the services but neither of them wanted breakfast. They were saving themselves for a late pub lunch, which Jane and Joe had promised at the Rope and Anchor - Sophie's favourite place for pub grub. The Rope and Anchor was run by Jane and Joe's closest friends Jon and Brenda. Jon was ex R.A.F and Brenda, before retiring, had run her own catering company for years. The couple had arrived in Devon about five years ago. The pub had been put up for auction, as the people who had owned it previously had run into financial difficulties. The previous owners had come from the city and didn't have a clue how to run a country pub. Well, that was according to the oracle of Jane.

They were just not cut out for country life. Too 'city', darling. They only lasted two years before they ran the place into the ground. Now then, Jon and Brenda, they had the right idea. Brenda is such a wonderful cook and Jon runs the place like one of his squadrons. Between them, they soon got the place back on its feet. The locals love Jon and his tales of the cold war and Brenda is such a darling. Everyone just adores them.

Granny Jane was not exaggerating; they were a lovely couple. They were both in their seventies. One would think that they would want to retire and enjoy a quieter life. Instead, they sold their large family home in Berkshire. Their son had left home years earlier to relocate to Scotland. They had long since given up hope that he would one day move back to the Berkshire area. They made a bid on the pub and had thrown themselves into a new challenge. The rest was history. They were inspiring for any person over a certain age. They seemed to thrive on hard work. The Rope and Anchor had converted a couple of their spare rooms and offered Bed and Breakfast. Joe and Jane would call Jon and Brenda if they were fully booked and they would take the over spill from The Sand Banks, and vice versa. It was a good arrangement and Sophie was happy that her granny and gramps had made good friends so close by.

'It's this next turnoff. We don't go far before we hit the coastal road so keep your eyes open to your left -hand side; you will see it once we clear the forest. The view is breath-taking.'

Sophie's mind wandered back to another journey, a year or so back with her ex, Danny. Sophie was head over heels in love with Danny. They had met at the Gym. A bit of a cliché really. Their eyes had met over the bubbles of the Jacuzzi. They'd both been drinking coffee in the bar after their respective workouts and had struck up a conversation. He had been older, an accountant and very sophisticated, totally gorgeous. He had wined her, dined her, made her laugh and made her happy in the bedroom department. They were seeing each other for about twelve months and then he had started to become distant. Sophie had questioned him as to why he was not seeing as much of her as he had been doing. He had made excuses that he had been busy with work. He had also told her that his father had not been too well. That part had been true, at least. Sophie decided that a few days away would do them good and so she had pestered him until he agreed to take time out for them. They arranged a couple of nights in a swanky hotel and had arranged to drop in overnight first at her grans, only they never got there. They had stopped at the same services on the way down she and Stevie had just stopped at and Danny had left her in the car and gone in to grab some flowers for her gran. That was Danny all over. He had only just gone into the service station when Sophie saw he had left his swanky new mobile phone on the driver's seat. It had rung and Sophie did not think twice about answering it.

'Hello, Danny's phone.'

'Hello, who's that?' A woman asked from the other end.

'It's Sophie. Danny will be back in a moment. Can I tell him who has called?'

'Oh Sophie, you must be Danny's new secretary. Just tell him to call his wife back please, it's urgent. His father has taken a turn for the worse. He will have to cancel his meetings and come straight to the hospital.'

With that the woman had ended the call. Sophie couldn't believe it. A wife. Married. It was unreal. It could not be happening. When he returned to the car, Sophie gave Danny precisely the correct message as passed onto her by his wife.

'Oh my god, Sophie, who did you say you were?'

Sophie had just looked at him in utter disgust and disbelief.

'Fortunately for you, she assumed I was your bloody secretary.'

He had been so sorry, blah, blah and bloody blah. He had been meaning to tell her. He hadn't meant to hurt her and was initially intending to leave his wife for her but then Harriet had found out she was pregnant. His father was ill. It was all too much for him. He really was so sorry. He was going to tell me this weekend; he was just waiting to find the right moment.

What a bloody gentleman! Sophie, with as much dignity as she could muster, had climbed out of the passenger seat and got her overnight bag from the boot. With bag in hand, she had leaned down and said through the open driver's window...

'Good bye then, Danny. Good luck and god help your wife, that's all I have to say to you.'

He wasted no time in starting the engine and pulling off into the traffic, leaving her stood there in total shock. Sophie had been forced to call her grandparents and explain that she was stranded about an hour and a half away and could her gramps pick her up. Sophie had felt sick, utterly betrayed and very stupid. It was more than three hours later that she had eventually arrived, rather forlornly, at Sand Banks. Gran had been totally wonderful and had held her and let her ramble on, soaking her with tears and snot. Her gran had just stroked her hair and let her cry. Eventually, as she lay there, totally emotionally spent, she had gently pushed her away from her and taken her two hands in her own and asked her to listen carefully.

'Sweetheart, I know right now you feel completely empty and devastated. Life does that to us. Then, just when we think that it cannot get any worse, it sometimes does. That means that, if it can do worse to us, it can also get better. Sometime in the future you will look on this as a mere blip. You can either give up or darned well get on with it. Only we ourselves have that choice.'

Some bloody big blip, she'd thought at the time. After Danny had played her for the naive fool she had been, Sophie had felt so empty and cross. However, she did make the decision that she would not let the experience make her bitter. Learn and move on. Hopefully without scaring any future man she met with endless questions about him being absolutely single.

Rounding the bend, breaking through the trees, the view just hit them. The sea that shone through the landscape was like a beautifully icy prism. Shades of deep and light blue sparkled across its rippled surface.

'Wow and double wow! That view is stunning. How could you say that this place was not my scene? You must have me down as a complete philistine you wicked girl. This place is fab-u-lous! It is totally breath-taking. I wish Jason could see this view. In fact, pull up where you can and let me take a pic?'

Sophie pulled the mini off the road into a small clearing, turned the engine off. Stevie jumped out and she followed him.

'It is lovely isn't it? I love the fact that all you can hear is the sounds of birds singing and the seagulls calling. It's heavenly. I always get that rush of excitement when I get to hear them and get that first glimpse of the sea.'

'It certainly is something. We gays are the masters at 'beauty appreciation'. I can't get over the fact that you thought this wouldn't be my scene.'

Sophie laughed out loud.

'Oh Stevie! It wasn't the beauty I thought was not you. It's the quietness of the lifestyle down here that I thought you may find too much.'

'Well, Miss Smarty Pants, let me be the judge of that. I can enjoy peace and quiet with the best of them. I just have my own way of livening things up when they get too quiet!' Stevie gave Sophie a mischievous look. She groaned.

'Come on, let's get going. We should get to Grans in about twenty minutes.'

The rest of the drive was done in quietness; they were both enjoying the beauty around them. Stevie caught his first glimpse of the local small village which housed a few gift shops and a couple of pubs, one of which was the Rope and Anchor. He loved it on sight and declared that he'd be happy to spend his days growing old in a place just like it. Sophie very much doubted this would be the case. After a few days here he would probably change his mind. She could never imagine even an old Stevie enjoying the quietness of this area for long. Taking a left-hand turn about a mile out of the village, they followed the lane around its twists and bends. They drove through a copse of pine trees which were dotted intermittently along the way. As the trees disappeared, they came upon their first glimpse of Sand Banks. It stood off to their left at the top of a large expanse of green lawn area. There was a grey pebbled driveway which wound up to the house, being flanked with a variety of rhododendrons and other shrubs. Set back were a variety of large oaks and elms, dramatically twisted and gnarled with age. The house looked out of place in this area, almost too grand. It had Georgian windows with Victorian features added at some later stage, or vice versa. As they drove closer, Stevie took in the details of the place. The ridge of the roof had blocks of stone across the perimeter which would be more in keeping with a castle. Grey slated roof tiles sloped up towards four large chimney stacks. The two story property was perfectly proportioned. Each level housed large Georgian windows, with yellow sandstone ledges at the base of each window, matching both upper and lower level. To the centre of the ground floor featured a rather imposing front entrance. Two sandstone pillars supported a covered porch. Three steps led up to a mosaic tiled entrance way. Large oak double fronted doors, with ornate stained glass, made a real statement. A larger window, on the centre upper floor, balanced the property perfectly. Some aspects of it reminded him of the architecture of many smaller castles dotted throughout the Scottish regions. Off to the right there was a large Victorian style orangery and just visible through the glass were an array of tropical plants, sympathetically creating a lovely space for a number of tables. This was where they served their breakfasts. Growing up, the left side of the house was a mass of wild roses and behind them was a trellis laden with wisteria, heavy with light lilac plumes. The first impression of the house was quite captivating.

As the mini pulled up, the front doors opened. A rather giddy golden retriever, named Eddie, bounded out, followed by Jane herself, looking every bit as giddy as her dog. Jane was wearing a pair of beige fitted jeans, a white shirt and a sleeveless, khaki green body warmer. The jeans surprisingly didn't look out of place on a woman of her age, as she had kept the shape of a much younger woman. Her silvered hair was upswept into a rather elegant French pleat and her face was flushed with excitement.

'Sophie, darling, here you are. Eddie heard your car before I did and nearly knocked me off my feet in his excitement to greet you. Joe is out back, watering his Geraniums,' Jane turned her attention to Stevie, 'Hello there, you must be Sophie's friend, Stevie. Lovely to meet you. Welcome to Sand Banks.' With gusto, Jane briskly walked over to Stevie and grabbed him by the hand shaking it exuberantly. Jane turned to hug Sophie briefly, planting a firm kiss on both of her cheeks.

'This is a beautiful place you have here Mrs…,' she cut him short.

'Call me Jane, dear. No formalities here.'

'It's stunning. Just stunning, Jane.'

'Well, we think so! Don't we, Sophie? Now come on, don't let's just stand here, get your bags out and leave them at the desk in the hall and we can have some tea. Joe is so excited about your visit. He can't wait to see you, Sophie.' With that, Jane pulled open the boot of the mini and started to unload the two bags in there.

'Let me do that, Jane. Sophie's is heavy.'

'Oh, how lovely, a gentleman! So rare these days. This way, Stevie.' Jane strode off, grabbing Sophie and propelling her by the hand up the steps and into the Hallway. 'Just there, dear, by the desk. Follow us through to the gardens.'

Stevie dropped the bags by the desk, taking in his surroundings as he followed Jane and Sophie through the magnificent mosaic tiled hallway. It was larger than the lounge in his flat. The huge reception desk, made of carved oak, was situated at the bottom of an imposing staircase. It climbed gently to a half landing, splitting in two directions up to the gallery above. The wide steps were carpeted in deep red, held in place by brass grips on each side of the runner. Two large doors were situated off from either side of the hallway. Stevie could only catch a glimpse of them as he hurried after the two women. They disappeared through another door, which led off to a smaller corridor behind the desk. An aroma of roses, mixed with old wood and furniture polish, floated on the air, emanating from the large vase of flowers proudly displayed on the reception desk.

'Joe!!! Joe, darling, our beautiful Sophie has arrived with her friend Stevie. Joe, where are you?'

Jane briskly led them through a drawing room, with purposeful strides, to a wide set of French windows, leading onto a patio which ran the full length of the house. As Stevie emerged onto the patio, it completely took his breath away. A massive expanse of lush green lawn, boarded by a variety of flowers, gently undulated down to an uninterrupted view of sea and coastland. Sophie caught Stevie's expression.

'Breath-taking, isn't it? I'll take you for a stroll over to the end of the garden after tea. You will see why Gran and Gramps have called it Sand Banks. There are some steps at the bottom of the garden which lead down between the dunes and onto our very own bit of beach below. It's a very beautiful hidden cove. You can't see it from here.'

'Sophie, sweet-heart, give your old granddad a big hug.'

A rather jolly-looking, scruffy, older gentleman trotted over as fast as his small bandy legs would take him. He was not at all what Stevie had expected. He didn't look like the sort of chap he would have imagined married to Jane. He grabbed Sophie in a big bear hug and, after releasing her, took Stevie by his hand, nearly shaking it off in his enthusiasm. He turned his attention back to his granddaughter.

'Well, well, about time you came to see us both. Your grandmother has barely been able to sleep for excitement the last couple of nights. How was the journey? You're earlier than we expected.'

'We set off quite early, Gramps, to avoid traffic. The drive was fine, no holdups. How have you been keeping? The garden's look lovely by the way.'

'Fine, just fine. A few stiff joints here and there but nothing much to complain about really. You can't expect not to have the odd ache here and there at our time of life can you, eh Jane?'

'Speak for yourself. My joints are perfectly fine, thank you very much. So don't include me in that.'

Sophie laughed.

'I see you two are still the same as ever. It's so lovely that nothing changes.'

The couple both smiled affectionately at each other and Joe gave Sophie a little wink.

'Let me go and get washed up and changed whilst you have some tea and then I expect you two will be hungry. We can go and get some lunch.'

'I was hoping you would suggest that, Gramps. I told Stevie all about the lovely food at Jon and Brenda's pub. We've saved our appetites for it.'

'Smashing, that's sorted then. A good old pub lunch it is.' Joe grabbed Sophie again in another bear hug and then tottered off to get changed.

CHAPTER 18

Ann

Scotland
Aug 1996

ANN WAS CLEARING out Ailsa's old bedroom. It was high time she sorted her stuff into boxes and redecorated the room. It had been empty for a couple of years and now it was time to accept that she would only be back for the odd weekend. Ann was extremely proud of her, thinking back to the first time she had left home to go to University in Leeds, even though she had wept all the way home.

It had been hard at the time seeing her little girl walking away from her into her new accommodation; she'd looked so small and lost. She had tried to be brave saying her goodbyes. It had made Ann feel physically ill to the pit of her stomach to leave her. If it weren't for the strong presence of Ewan that day, she wouldn't have managed to pull herself away and be strong for them both. It seemed such a long time ago and looking back, rather silly of her to get so upset. It was the most natural thing in the world to let your children fly the nest.

Ewan had been the one blessing to have come out of the misery since Susan had been taken from her that fateful day, now so many years ago. Ewan was her rock that kept all the small stones in place. It had taken too long to escape the misery of her marriage to Stu. She had made countless excuses for his behaviour over the years, following the loss of their second child. He had drowned his sorrows in booze. It had escalated from beer to whiskey and, with the whiskey, the abuse had also escalated. It had started with the blame of her leaving the pram unattended, to coldness and indifference towards her. He would say terrible things to her that she couldn't un-hear. The physical abuse followed soon after. From the throwing of things, to the shoving and, eventually, the beatings. It had carried on and on and she had stupidly put up with it for about eight years.

Eventually, Ann had snapped. It was when Stu had really lost his temper with Ailsa for breaking a vase by accident. He had slapped her so hard that he had knocked her off her feet into the sideboard and split her lip. Ailsa had not stopped shaking and apologising, sobbing her heart out in her room all night. She'd told Ann she hadn't meant to be clumsy and make her dad angry, she had tried to avoid her father when she could but sometimes found it hard. It was one thing dealing with his irrational, abusive behaviour herself, but she couldn't allow her only child to live in fear of her own father. He had crossed a line hitting Ailsa the way he had. She had to protect them both before he killed one of them. God knows she'd tried. She had encouraged him to get help, begged him, even, but he was too far gone with the drinking and had crossed too many lines. He'd lost numerous jobs turning up at work still smelling sour from drinking the night before, with the sour temper to match. It was no wonder he could not hold down a job for long. After deliberating about how to do it, she'd called Evie the friendly P.C who had been on her case to get rid of Stu for as long as she could remember. Evie had been wonderful. At her suggestion, she had arranged for Ailsa to go to a friend's house from school overnight. She remembered how she had confided in the child's mother Hazel, who hadn't been shocked by what Ann told her. Apparently, half the village knew about Stuart's temper and drinking. Evie had suggested that Ann pack a bag for Stuart, essentials only, and have it ready by the front door. He could collect the rest of his things later. Ann had tried to leave Stu on a previous occasion and that had led to her taking a severe beating. This was her home. She had Ailsa to think about. She intended to stay put this time. Evie had said that Ewan Edwards, whom she knew already, had offered to be parked outside when she asked Stuart to leave, in case there was any trouble. As it turned out, he had surprised her. He said that he thought it was for the best as well. He went without even a raised eyebrow. At the time, she had been too shocked to question his reaction. It was only later that she learned that he'd been seeing a widow from the next village who had welcomed him with open arms. Unfortunately for the widow, Stuart had only stayed long enough to get her into debt. He then went on to charm his way into a long list of other women's affections. None of the relationships lasted. Stuart's drinking became worse and ill health took over. He ended up in a bedsit, all alone. He died of liver failure at the age of thirty-two.

It had been difficult for Ann when she heard. On the one hand, she was relieved that he was gone but, at the same time, she was sad. His alcoholism was a slow and painful way to go. Fortunately for Ann and Ailsa, they had avoided the last painful years of seeing Stuart suffer. His contact with Ailsa had become less frequent. He had only visited once in the two years prior to his death, looking more for a hand- out than being there to see his daughter, sadly. Although they were divorced and Ann had no legal obligation, she had arranged and paid for the funeral. He'd still been the father of her child.

Since he had left, Ann had taken on work sewing at home. It started as a way to get by but she had found that she had a real talent for it. She worked long hours, sometimes into the night but made good money. The most lucrative jobs were the wedding dresses she made. It had started with doing alterations for a bridal boutique in town but she quickly got a reputation for bespoke wedding dresses.

That was the start of how Ann and Ewan had become more than just friends. He was the one that arrived at the house to break the news that Stuart had been found dead in his bedsit. He had been tasked with looking into his 'sudden death'. He had been dead for five days before his body had been found. It was a sad fact that he had become invisible to people. All his friends, most of which had been drinking 'buddies', had dropped off one by one.

Ewan had popped around from time to time after Stuart had left and they had politely chatted about this and that, about how Ailsa was coping without having a dad around, and how Ann was coping, but there had never been anything intimate between them until the day of Stuart's funeral. That had been an evening to remember, Ann thought with a smile on her face. Ailsa had gone to her friends after the funeral, to have pizza and a sleepover with Amy, Hazel's daughter. Hazel and Ann thought it would be good for the two friends to do something normal and girlie at the end of such a difficult day for the child. Ann had been invited for a glass of wine by Hazel, but she had declined as she wanted to get home and be by herself, or so she thought. Ewan had generously taken a day off work to go with her and Ailsa to the funeral. After having dropped Ailsa at her friends, he'd then driven Ann home. They had pulled up outside the house and he had gone around to open the car door for her. At that precise moment, Ann had not wanted to be alone, despite what she had first thought; she needed company. Ann still remembered their conversation standing on the pavement.

'It was kind of you, Ewan. You've been a good friend to Ailsa and me. I thought I wanted my own company but right now it's the last thing I want. Do you need to get back or can you spare the time for a coffee or something a little stronger?'

'Now something a little stronger sounds a good idea. I've nowhere I need to be right now.'

He'd followed her into the house. Something was hanging in the air between them that day that hadn't been there before. There was a slight nervous tension. Ann had unlocked the door and Ewan had followed her. They both took off their respective coats in silence, barely making eye contact.

'I've only wine in. I won't have any spirits in the house,' Ann stated.

'Just a small glass. I'm driving.'

That was so typically Ewan, looking back, ever the sensible policeman. Ann had poured them both a drink and they had sat down together on the sofa. She'd smiled at him whilst taking a sip, not quite meeting his eye. She'd felt quite shy having him so close. Normally they'd sit in the kitchen when he would call around. The sofa had felt more intimate. Ewan had finished his drink and set aside the glass on the table at the side of him.

'Ailsa seemed to handle the day very well. What do you think?'

'I think she handled it all very well. The fact that Stuart was a missing link the last few years made it easier for her. They didn't really have any sort of relationship that a father and daughter should've had, as you know. I guess it was easier for her than me.'

'Yes. It must have been hard. He was still your children's father and I suppose there must have been some good times? How do you feel now it's over?'

Ann was quiet for a minute. 'Sad, resigned...but most of all, relieved.' Ann had then looked up into his eyes, her own, misted over with tears. The last time he'd seen her cry had been back when he'd brought Susie's blanket back. His thumb had gently brushed away a tear that had rolled down her cheek, he'd run his fingers along the contour of her face. He had slowly moved towards her, not breaking eye contact. His lips tenderly met hers and she had felt herself being drawn like a fraying thread that is pulled and unravels. His kiss was gentle but passionate. She'd found herself responding. First, tenderly, and then more urgently; the memory of it still made her blush. His lips had felt hot but so soft and wonderful. Ann had felt electricity coursing through her body. She'd felt a tingle that went straight from her stomach and lower, until it almost reached her toes. It was an electric feeling. She hadn't had this sort of reaction from her body before. They'd both kissed with hunger and need for each other, their breath hot. They had both moaned with the delight they found from each other's touch. Ann did not even know at what point they had undressed each other but they had found themselves on the floor naked and exhausted after their love making, grinning like a couple of teenagers. That had been the start, that late afternoon. They had both spent the night in bed and taken their time exploring each other's bodies and talking about how they had arrived at that point. Ewan had told her how he had never expected that anything would happen between them. He'd become aware his feelings for her deepening from the time he'd started dropping by to check she was okay after Stuart had left. She'd admitted that she'd been attracted to him since then too, but had thought that he was involved with Evie and had mistaken his visits for kindness, so she had never entertained any such thoughts further. He'd laughed at this and explained that Evie was not his type and although she may be attractive, he'd never felt that way towards her. They laughed and talked into the early hours of the morning, only sleeping for a couple of hours. After that, there was no stopping the emotions that took hold. They grew at a galloping rate.

Now here she was all these years later, married to him. It hadn't taken him long to ask. Only a year after that first passionate encounter. He moved her and Ailsa into his house with him. The fact that he loved and cared for them so tenderly was more than enough and she had readily agreed. Ewan made her feel safe and content. He also made her laugh. Especially when he was with Ailsa; he was always acting the fool around her. He said he loved to see her giggle and chuckle. The two of them had become quite close over the last few years. He was a good father to Ailsa and a good husband to her. At times like this, she thought how it would have been the four of them if Susie had been part of it, but then if Susie was alive, she would never had met him. If she was honest, if she could turn the clock back, she would have given up her own happiness in a heartbeat to not leave her in the pram that day. It didn't do to dwell; it wasn't healthy.

Her mind wandered back to the university days again. Ewan had been the one to drive Ailsa all over the country to look at various Unis. Ann herself had sometimes gone with them and sometimes not. She'd had a part time job at the time - in the local cafe bar - and with her shifts it was not always convenient. The sewing at home had been hard work on her hands and eyes, so Ann only did an occasional wedding dress for the right price to keep her hand in. She enjoyed the café; it was sociable and she enjoyed chatting with the customers.

After a lot of deliberation, Ailsa had settled on Leeds as her first option and was delighted that she was accepted. Ailsa had worked hard for her A Levels and had attained more than enough with her grades to get on the course for a degree in Modern Art and Design. After initially being very homesick for the first three weeks, Ailsa had taken to University life like a duck to water. Although she was a bubbly, chatty girl, she was not always confident when first meeting new people. It was Ewan who had advised her how to make friends. *Everybody is homesick and out of their comfort zone the first few days. If you knock on a few doors and introduce yourself, you will be surprised how easy it will be. Whoever answers the door, nine times out of ten they will be feeling as much a fish out of water as you are.* He had been right; Ailsa called and said she had done just that. The first door she had knocked on had been a girl from Devon. Together, they had knocked on a few more doors until they had met practically everyone on their floor. Ann did not have any experience of University life so she was pleased that Ewan could guide Ailsa this way. University had been a mixed bag for Ailsa. There had been: friendships made; friendships broken; tears after breakups with boyfriends and laughter on drunken nights out. The drinking was something that worried Ann a great deal, given Ailsa's father's history. Ewan assured Ann that it was just something Ailsa would do as a student and that it was just part of growing up. Still, it had worried Ann and she had frequently reminded Ailsa not to go overboard and drink plenty of water. For all her worrying, Ailsa had come out none the worse and a lot wiser. Having met different people from different financial and social backgrounds, it had given her a much more open mind. Ailsa grew an awful lot while she was away and came back home a much more mature Ailsa. Luck was also on her side as she got a job, almost immediately, in a studio in Glasgow so she was not home for more than about ten weeks. Almost immediately, she was sharing a flat in Glasgow with another girl in the same field of work and quite the independent lady.

Ailsa had met Max about two years later at an Art Exhibition. She had done the designs for the invitations and some other branding work for them. It was the sort of work which left Ann quite confused about exactly what art was. A lot of Ailsa's work was way over her head. Max was one of the contemporary artists who were showing their work at the exhibition. He lived and worked in Manchester. They had struck up an animated and intense conversation that had ended up in an exchange of phone numbers. After that, a long distance relationship was struck up and it soon became obvious to the young couple that one of them would have to make the move to be with the other. The trouble was that they were both passionate about their work and both quite stubborn about making the move. Eventually, it was made easier when Ailsa's studio got into financial difficulty and gave notice to their staff that their jobs would not be there for long. Ailsa had come home for a couple of weeks when it closed as she could not afford to keep her flat share. Not long after that, after much nagging from Max, she decided to move to Manchester.

That had been six months ago, thought Ann. She was now sharing a flat with Max and was helping him to market his work, whilst freelancing as an illustrator and designer. Ann was still mystified by what exactly her daughter did, as her design work was very diverse. They had a small studio space around the corner from their flat in Fallowfield and were building up a good reputation. They worked well together. Ann sometimes worried that working and living together could lead to difficulties but to date that did not seem to be an issue for them. She realised that she worried far too much. Ailsa had to make her own choices whether they be right or wrong. That was part of life. Part of being a mother meant letting them go but she had really struggled. She knew better than anyone that it was too easy to take your eye off the ball and things could go badly wrong.

Ann had never forgotten that awful day, so many years ago. Her mistake, lack of judgment or whatever you could call it, was etched into her very soul. It had left a nasty scar - the sort of scar that sometimes would erupt and itch and drive her crazy. She never let Ailsa or Ewan know how deep that scar still went. Time is supposed to be a great healer but some things will never heal. Ann tried to take comfort from the child she had left. Ailsa was the only reason that she had managed to get up and out of bed each morning in the early years after it happened. Not one day or night went past, even now, that she did not think about Susan and how stupid she had been to leave her outside in her pram that day. It was still like an ache in her gut whenever she passed a pram, even now, years later. Maybe Ewan had caught the look in her eye at those times but there had never been talk of her and Ewan having a child of their own. She thought he understood, without any discussion, that she could never have done it. Some people, she supposed, would have done. It may even have filled that hole they felt, a little, but it wasn't for her.

There had been a time, in the early years, when Ailsa had caught Ann in the bedroom with a box that contained some items that had been Susan's. Ann knew it was not healthy to keep them but it was all she had left of her. She had not heard Ailsa creeping up beside her. It was then that she had to explain to Ailsa why she had the tiny items. *They were your baby sisters, Susan.* Ann had explained. *Oh Mummy, don't be sad, she is happy where she is.* It was a strange thing for her to have said. Children put things so simply. Ann had just smiled, put the lid back on the box, pulled Ailsa close to her and revelled in the smell of her beautiful daughter. She supposed that Ailsa had meant with the angels. They had been doing a lot in school about God, Jesus and angels. It had been that time of year when the nativity rehearsals were in full swing.

There had only been a couple of conversations about Susan with Ailsa since that day and it had been when Ailsa was about fifteen. They had been talking in school about one of the girls in their year that had been missing for a few days. The girl in question had been found safe, at a boyfriend's house. She'd ended up in a lot of trouble for wasting police time and for causing her parents such anxiety. Ailsa had come home and asked about the details of her sister's disappearance and how she had felt. Ann had tried to be factual and honest. It had been a painful conversation to have. They had both ended up crying and hugging.

It hadn't been mentioned again, until two years later when Ailsa had questioned her mother again. This time she wanted to know more about the woman that had taken Susan. This conversation had been prompted by a paper she was writing as part of her sociology A Level coursework, on postnatal depression. Thankfully for Ann, that had been it. No more questions. Ailsa had been of an age that she had some understanding how deeply painful Ann's memories were.

It was still there though, every day, that yearning to turn the clock back and make a different decision. Life wasn't like that though; you had to make the best of what you had and be grateful. She was lucky to have one healthy child and Ailsa had given her so much joy over the years and she had her lovely Ewan. It was more than she felt she deserved. The loss of Susan was her pain, alone, to bear.

Ann was still in Ailsa's room an hour later when she heard Ewan's key in the front door.

'Up here in Ailsa's room,' she shouted down.

As he arrived at the door of Ailsa's room, he had to smile. She'd been clearing this room out for the past few months, with a view to redecorate and all that seemed to happen was that Ailsa's belongings got shunted around but it never looked any clearer than the day Ann had started. He had to smile to himself; he loved this woman so much it made his gut ache. He'd never thought he would ever pluck up the courage to make a move but in the end it was unexpected and felt totally natural. He felt now, looking at her, that it was as if she had always been his. Ann was a striking looking woman. Her curly dark brown hair fell in gentle waves just past her shoulders; the light from the window picked out the auburn glints that ran through it. Her large round hazel eyes showed little signs of her age. At nearly forty-eight, she still had the body of a thirty-year old. He was one 'lucky son of a gun' and he knew it. They had been together for a few years now and he marvelled at how amazing the love making still was. It just seemed to get better and better. After that first frantic time they had had sex, Ann had been quite shy about her body in front of him but now he knew every inch of her, even down to a small heart shaped mole on the inside of her right thigh. Ann turned to see Ewan with a daft grin on his face.

'What?'

'Are you ever actually going to move any of these boxes into the loft or shall we redecorate and put all of Ailsa's things back where they are?' Ewan laughed as he asked her, pulling her up into his arms.

'I know it's completely stupid. I can't believe it's taking me so long. I have six boxes ready to go up there. I mean it isn't as though we will never see her again. It's just harder than I thought it would be. I've decided to leave a few of her personal things here, though. For when she comes back for visits. I want her to know it's still her home and that this is still her room.'

'I'm sure she'll be back plenty,' he reassured her. 'Manchester's not the other side of the world, you know. She hasn't lived at home for the last few years and has been back and forth.'

'Well, she was closer then. Manchester seems a lot further away and now she's met Max and is helping run the business; I doubt they will have the time to visit.'

'The idea was to redecorate the room and replace the single bed with a double, just for that very reason. When Ailsa comes home for a visit, which she will, Max will probably come too.'

'You're right. I'm just being totally ridiculous. Right,' Ann said decisively, 'as you're here, you can take these boxes up to the loft and dismantle the bed and we can call the charity shop and get them to collect it. The mattress can go to the tip.' Ann kissed Ewan firmly on the lips and they set about moving the boxes into the hallway.

CHAPTER 19

Ailsa

Manchester
Aug 1996

'BLOODY HELL MAX. What are you playing at? I nearly broke my ruddy neck on those boxes, you plonker,' Ailsa shouted.

Not for the first time, Ailsa asked herself what she had been thinking of, moving in with this disorganised, lazy man who drove her crazy. Why? Because for all that, she had to admit to herself, he was bloody amazing in other areas. She rubbed the shin of her right leg, which had caught the edge of a pile of boxes. Boxes that had been left right in the entrance of the hallway just inside the front door. Ailsa clambered over the boxes, throwing her door keys onto the hall table and made her way into their pokey kitchen come diner/living room. Max was nowhere in sight.

'Max! Max, where are you?'

There was no answer. Typical. Leaves the T.V blasting and he's not even in. Flopping down on the threadbare sofa, she kicked off her shoes.

Her feet were killing her; she had traipsed all around Didsbury this morning, delivering leaflets through the doors of homes that looked affluent. Then, she had caught a bus into Manchester.

Manchester was where it was all happening. The music industry was thriving. New clubs were popping up everywhere. She had traipsed around offices, shops, pubs and clubs, delivering loads of leaflets. There were blisters on her blisters. She looked down at her feet. Yuk. She really needed to sort out that chipped nail polish and give her feet a good soak. He would think she had let herself go just because they had moved in together. Slippery slope and all that. Ailsa also looked down at the scruffy jeans she had been wearing and groaned. New clothes - she really needed some new clothes. Lord, she looked more like a scruffy student now, than when she was one, back in the day. The exhibition was only a week away but there was still so much to do. She didn't have anything decent to wear. You couldn't introduce yourself as a professional designer and businesswoman looking like a tramp, she told herself.

Ailsa went over to the fridge, which was a short stride from the sofa, and opened it. For the love of God; there was cold dried- up curry, with the sauce congealed to the side of the dish, a shrivelled up cucumber, half a tomato and a tin of beans (opened) with spoon sticking out. Gross. However, all was not lost, Ailsa spied a dish of cold pasta next to an empty milk carton. She grabbed the dish and a spoon from the drainer and shovelled it down. Discarding the empty dish into the sink, she crossed the living room to the bedroom, which was only a few more strides from the couch than the fridge was.

Unbelievable! It was a hovel. The bed was as it had been this morning when they had gotten out of it, except there was now a wet bath towel left in the middle of it. The curtains were still partly shut and partly hanging off their hooks. Max had been promising to re-hang them for ages. The chest of drawers was cluttered with both their things but Max had obviously been looking for something because half the contents of the drawers lay strewn out of them and across the floor. The wardrobe doors stood open with half of the clothes hanging off some of the hangers and the rest of the contents lay in a dishevelled mess on the bottom of the wardrobe floor. *Welcome home Ailsa*, she muttered to herself. With a huff, she stripped off her jeans, tee-shirt and undies, and strolled across the room to the bathroom. It was en-suite. Well, it was off the bedroom anyway. Ailsa thought it was probably originally a storage cupboard in the bedroom. Bathroom was not a term that applied to this room. It just about held a loo, a shower and a small wash basin.

The water was lukewarm but very pleasant. Ailsa grabbed the shower gel and worked it to a soapy lather and massaged it into her aching muscles.

'Why not let me do that for you. I'm sure I could make it much more pleasurable for you.'

Ailsa hadn't heard Max come in and it made her jump. Then, she felt his hands. One cupped around her left breast, whilst his right hand had moved gently around the front of her, stroking her stomach. Max had somehow managed to creep into the bathroom, undress and sneak into the shower behind her, without her hearing him. Ailsa felt his tongue and lips on the back of her neck, working gently towards her ear. He manoeuvred her expertly around to face him and continued to kiss her neck, face and lips. Ailsa felt the passion and need in him increasing with the pressure of his kisses. He pushed her further back against the tiles so he could take control of her. She moved her body to accommodate the need in Max to enter her and felt him there almost too quickly. He was eager and she gave into him quite happily. Max did not waste much time once he had entered her; he had climaxed almost immediately then leaned against her breathing heavily.

'Ohhhh baby, you're so hot. I just couldn't stop myself.'

'God, you're a right bastard. You really know how to make an entrance, no pun intended! You know I can't shout at you now for not tidying up before you went out.'

'What me, do that? That would be so premeditated. I'm hurt you would suggest such a thing. Anyway, how can I resist shagging you if I see you in the shower like that?'

'No need to be coarse.'

'Sorry my sweet, how can I resist making love to you?'

'Seriously Max. I hate it when you are coarse; you make me feel awful.'

'Come on hon, lighten up, you and your Catholic guilt. Sex is good, not bad, and just because we enjoy it, doesn't mean we can't joke about it. You know I love the bones of you.'

Ailsa laughed and gave Max a playful slap.

'I know, I know, it's just me. I love sex but I hate the word shag. You know I'm not catholic - it's just the way I was brought up.'

'Your mum and dad aren't prudes. I bet they're at it all the time. I've seen the way they look at each other, even if they don't swear.'

"Yuk. Do you have to put that image in my head? Anyway, forget my parent's sex life. I don't suppose you have brought home any food with you to feed me, have you?'

'It so happens I have. I stopped at the shops on my way home.'

'You mean you left the TV on since this morning?'

'Oops, did I? Sorry, I got caught up on the phone and had to rush. There was a delivery due and I thought I was going to miss it.'

'Never mind, but Max, please try and remember that it all costs and we can't afford to waste money on burning electricity for the sake of it.'

'Yes marm. Sorry marm. Won't happen again marm.'

Ailsa laughed again and this time pushed him away to finish her shower.

Both having showered, they were sat down eating spaghetti Bolognese and chilling in front of the TV less than an hour later.

'I had a really exciting call this morning. There is an exhibition in Manchester being planned for early next year. I have been asked if I would like to exhibit a conceptual piece of work,' Max said.

'Okay and why is that so exciting? Given that you often get asked to display your sculptures on a fairly regular basis?'

He turned to her with a look in his eyes which not only reflected his excitement but held a shifty look as well. Ailsa was sure something more was going on.

'Christine Hancock is the organiser and she only displays the best work. Plus, her connections can lead places, not to mention the elite guest list. You can just smell the money. This could mean a tasty size commission, or more, if I'm lucky.'

So that was it: bloody Christine Hancock! Ailsa should have known. That look of excitement was shifty. She knew she had recognised that look.

Christine Hancock was a rich daddy's girl, who got her kicks by sticking out her large chest and purring at any man that took her fancy. What Christine wanted, Christine got. She loved the fact that blokes couldn't resist her. The last time that Max had been involved in one of her exhibitions, she was sure that something more had gone on between them. It had caused a lot of angst at the time but she really hadn't any proof to back up her suspicions, so she had no choice but to drop it.

'Oh great. Her, again. Every man's dream woman. Except for the venom she carries with her.'

'For Christ-sake, Ailsa, not that again. Can't you just be pleased for me? It's not my fault she looks so fucking incredible. It's just work and I can't afford to turn work down because you're so bloody paranoid and insecure.'

'Great. Fucking incredible looking, is she? Is that why you enjoyed having her all over you the last time? Which by the way, you bloody well loved, so don't deny it.'

'I absolutely didn't encourage her. You know damn well it's just the way she works. Christine is like that with all guys. It's harmless. Anyway, why the hell would I go there with what we have?'

'Yeah right, except that you seemed to spend far too much time in discussions over lunch last time, which was totally unnecessary.'

'I'm not going through all that shit again, Ailsa. You are so over-reacting. It's work and nothing else. Anyway, who turns down a free lunch and a few beers? She was paying. I can't afford to pick and choose who I work with.'

Ailsa knew she would not win this argument and she'd wanted a nice, relaxed night in. Bloody Christine Hancock was not going to ruin that as well. This time she would keep an extra close eye on the man-eating witch. That was for sure. There was no way she was going to allow herself to be made a fool of. Ailsa had given him the benefit of the doubt last time but there was absolutely no way on god's earth she would do that again. She let it drop and turned back to her food. It was good and she wasn't having her evening spoilt by talking about that woman. Ailsa was a good cook, having learnt from her mother, who was brilliant. One thing that Max loved was his food. Ailsa loved seeing him eat and he always asked for seconds. He was like a little boy. Sometimes, if it was something that was his favourite, he would sneak out of bed in the morning and finish it off for breakfast.

Ailsa, not for the first time that day, looked around their flat. It was so utterly depressing. There was nothing at all that reflected either of their personalities. It looked like it had been furnished from the contents of the local charity shop. Nothing matched and it all looked rather tired and worn out. The television took ten minutes to warm up, not that they watched much T.V. The kitchen table was covered in rings of stains from cups placed on it that were too hot. The four chairs surrounding it were all odd and had horrible scratch marks on the legs. The kitchen units looked like they were a throwback to the seventies and half the cupboard doors were either hanging off or did not shut at all. Somebody had tried to make them look a little more 'nineties' and had painted them a petrol blue eggshell but they were chipped in various places. The best thing was the fridge freezer they had bought together. Even that looked a mess, as it was covered in papers held in place by magnets and post it stickers. The rest of the room had a collection of items which Max had brought home with the intention of using them for one of his sculptures but they had never found their way to his workshop come studio. Ailsa felt her spirits deflate at the thought of having to spend many more weeks in this excuse for a home. They had been in the flat for about six months. It was their first home together and they were saving up a deposit for a bigger place - one that would give them more space. The deposit they would get back from this place was pennies compared to what they would need for something bigger. They would also need to find more money for rent. Things were tight. They really did have to watch every penny. With a bit of luck, in the New Year they would have enough saved to consider moving and could start looking for somewhere. By then, they both hoped the business would be doing a bit better. Alisa herself had picked up a couple of regular clients, who were now using her as their regular designer. Should she be able to get another couple of regulars, things would really improve for them financially. Max had had some luck too. His name was getting out there. He had a couple of commissions for pieces from the 'Cheshire set', as Ailsa called them. Some of them had more money than sense. Ailsa felt slightly guilty for having a go at him. Max's work was brilliant but even though she loved him, she wouldn't pay two thousand for a piece of his art or anyone else's for that matter. Still, if they wanted to spend that amount, great. They would get a new place all the sooner. The lovely thing about the Cheshire set is their lovely 'top dog' attitude. If *so and so* had a piece of art, when it was seen by their friends, said friends wanted something to top it. It was wonderful for Max. The stupid thing is that the more expensive the piece, the more they wanted it. The more it cost the better the piece. These people weren't shy about bragging about the price tag - the higher the better. It was bonkers. Boring little people.

Ailsa's friend Sally noticed it when she had her first child. Having married a well to do solicitor, she mixed with the you-ha henrys and their wives. When she'd first had some of the fellow mums around, the women spent most of their time looking around Sally's beautiful home, asking where this was from and where that was from. They all started to copy and outdo the things she had. Apparently, it happened with children's birthday parties too. They all needed to compete with one another and have the most costly magician or entertainer etc. They must have nothing else going on in their lives, Ailsa had surmised. Crazy, crazy people.

Ailsa had not been around this area long enough to get her name out there. She was good and exhibitions were one of her favourite avenues of work. It was exciting to have free reign with your designs, making them reflect the different stuff being exhibited was a craft that not many people appreciated. It was not always as possible with the commercial stuff she did, as clients had very set ideas as to what they wanted. The Artist's often got her talent. This new exhibition would most certainly attract the right crowd but Ailsa could not help but worry. Christine Hancock meant trouble for her and Max's relationship and she could not help that niggle at the back of her mind that Max was as pleased about meeting up with her again, as he was about the possibility of the money it could bring in.

Food finished, Max washed up and they were soon snuggling up in bed together. They both had a lot to do the next day. Ailsa had to screen print some of the stuff for the exhibition, which was now six days away. Max had to finish one of the pieces that would be exhibited. Yes, they had a busy day ahead of them. It was thoughts of Christine Hancock primarily, that Ailsa had circling inside her head, like a swarm of wasps that stopped her sleeping.

CHAPTER 20

Carol

Yorkshire
Aug 1996

C AROL HAD NOT expected her doctor to send her for further tests. Usually, he just offered her anti-depressants and told her to keep taking them, not just stopping them as she had a habit of doing after a few weeks, when she felt better. This time had been different. He had said that the fact she was being sick, with blurred vision as well, was of concern to him. He wanted to send her for a scan. She was told that she would get an appointment quite quickly and not to worry. But, the last time that she had suffered a little light headedness after stopping taking the medication suddenly, she hadn't been sick in the way she had lately. The headaches had been there, on and off, for years. In truth, they had gotten quite intense recently. She had assumed it was just another side effect of her having stopped taking the pills again. The doctor said he didn't want to prescribe anything until he had the results from the scan. She was to just take paracetamol for the time being.

Carol meandered along the High Street, looking in shop windows at nothing in particular; her thoughts were all over the place. The day had turned out to be hot and clammy and she couldn't concentrate on anything. It had been her intention to treat herself to a new pair of Jeans on the way back from the doctors. Sophie had told her that she should treat herself to a bit of retail therapy to cheer herself up. She had been feeling her black moods dragging her down. Given that she had dropped nearly ten pounds in the last six weeks, Carol thought she might get away with trying to update her wardrobe a bit. She hadn't worn Jeans in years as she had felt too frumpy. Sophie was always saying she dressed too conservatively and should get a bit more 'with it'. Today she had woken feeling a bit more positive but now she could feel another headache coming on and she longed to just get home and lie down for a while. Plus, the High Street was too busy. The sun always seemed to bring more shoppers out. There was a group of teenagers walking towards her, laughing and clowning about. It made her yearn for the years back when Sophie was still at home. The house seemed too quiet without her there. She had too much time on her own to think about things, which always seemed to make her more agitated.

Carol picked up her pace and made her way through the happy shoppers and across the road to the car park. At first, she stood at the small, fenced barrier, unable to recollect where on earth she had parked the car. She had a complete blank moment; she couldn't even remember what car it was! *What was it? She couldn't even picture the colour, never mind the make.* It was a feeling of utter panic. *Ridiculous, stupid. How can you forget what car you drive?* She stood there, dumbstruck, with a bewildered look on her face for what seemed like minutes but was probably only seconds.

'Are you alright there, love? You look like you've lost a shilling and found a penny.'

Carol turned her attention to the voice of the parking attendant, which cut into her thoughts.

'Yes. Yes, thanks. Just having one of those moments. Can't remember which car I came into town with, mine or my husband's. Daft isn't it? It must be an age thing,' she said, trying to cover her complete memory loss. She felt acutely embarrassed and flushed, trying to keep the tremor out of her voice, a little close to tears in her confusion.

The attendant smiled at her kindly.

'Well, it so happens I can help you there. It was the blue Rover 2.5. I know that because my wife and I just got one last week. I wanted the blue and she wanted the red. We ended up getting the red. Have to say, I prefer the blue myself. Saw you parking it about an hour ago.'

'Of course! How daft of me. I've had so much to do I've been meeting myself coming back.'

Carol felt relief and gratitude flood over her at the attendant's words. They almost instantly helped her recollect the car she had been driving. The attendant was still talking about the argument he and his wife had over the colour of the car, as Carol scanned the car park for the car. It was parked directly one row in front of her, next to a silver BMW. Feeling more than a bit silly, she made her way to the car. The car park attendant carried on chatting away to her as she crossed to her parking space.

'I hope you enjoy driving your new car. My husband and I have been really pleased with our experience of it. Thanks for your help.'

'You're welcome. The wife's the same about forgetting things. It usually ends up being my fault, though, because I don't help her enough around the house and she's juggling too much.'

The attendant left her to her thoughts, walking away from her, laughing to himself and shaking his head.

She made it back home within about ten minutes. They lived in a quieter area, just outside the town centre. Turning into the drive, her home looked very welcoming at that moment and she couldn't wait to get in, make a cup of tea and take two pain killers. Bill would be in by five thirty and she wanted to prepare dinner. The poor man had cooked his own dinner the last couple of nights due to her head and she felt very guilty. It wasn't as though she had to work. Her only job the last few years had been keeping house. Bill had been a good provider; she wanted for nothing. Carol smiled at the thought of good dependable Bill. She still loved him as much, if not more than ever. With him being away a lot at the start of their marriage, it hadn't always been the happiest. It had been a rocky road in many ways but she pushed these thoughts to the very back of her mind as some things she couldn't change. She had made some tough decisions and there was no looking back. Some things had to be left buried.

Carol turned the key in the front door; there was a knack to it. They had meant to have the lock changed when they first moved in as it was stiff but they had never got around to it. The smell of the wood from the old piano standing in the hallway hit her. It made her feel safe and warm inside. It was the only thing her mother had let her have of her grandmother's, after she had died. Was it really thirty-two years ago? It must be. Her memories of her grandmother were still crystal clear, as if it had been only yesterday. She'd felt so close to her Gran and was sad that she didn't have the same strength of feeling for her Mum. Granny Grace had always been so warm and gentle. Memories of her playing dress up with her when she was small still filled her with warmth. Gran would pretend to be the prince and she was the princess. She would trot around in her gran's high heels and nylon under slip, which would come down to the floor on her. A nylon lace curtain would be pinned around her head, as if it were a veil. Loads of beads would be around her neck and she would parade around, giving orders to her prince. She laughed to herself at the memory of her gran with an umbrella for a sword and her drawn on moustache from an eye pencil. It was so much fun. She loved to play the piano for her whilst they would sing songs together. Then, her mother would turn up all fussy and spoil the fun because Carol wasn't dressed and ready to be collected. Time had run away from them. She'd be cross that she would be delayed getting her father's tea. Carol's mum was a stickler for time and routine. Her life was packed full to the brim and she had no time for a small child putting more demand on her due to *tardy behaviour*. She basically hadn't had the time or patience for her. Maybe that was why she had stopped at one.

Carol walked through to the lounge and put her bag on the sofa and her keys on the sideboard. Then, she went through to the kitchen to look in the fridge and decide what to prepare for Bill's tea. The fridge looked relatively empty compared to how it was usually stocked. There was some smoked salmon in the freezer and there was pasta, so she could knock up smoked salmon pasta with garlic bread. Bill would enjoy that. He often complimented her on her cooking skills. He loved plain wholesome food. Equally, he loved it when she tried something a bit different. She took the salmon out of the freezer and switched on the kettle to make her-self a cup of tea. Her head was really starting to pound now, despite having taken the pain killers. She decided against the tea and went upstairs to lie down. The curtains were still closed from the morning in the master bedroom, giving the room a warm orange glow. Being a south facing room, the sun shone in and made it very stuffy, even in the winter. Carol always, during sunny days, left the curtains closed all day, but she still needed to open two windows to let the gentle breeze cool the room.

She loved this bedroom. It was decorated with fine light oak modern furniture. The dressing table was built into the fitted wardrobes to make the most of the spacious room. It had a huge mirror above it which reached up the ceiling. The bed linen was an aqua green and there was a gold quilted bedspread which had been pulled back. It was piped in the same aqua green as the bedding and the curtains had been made to match. From her position on the bed, with her head resting up right on the plump pillows, she caught sight of her reflection in the dresser mirror. It was the face of a very tired woman. She hardly recognised herself as the young woman she had once been, before everything had changed. Things had never been the same for her since the accident, which was now well over twenty plus years ago. Each year the struggle to forget had become gradually harder. Her nerves had been stretched and inevitably the stress of that had, she thought, made her look older than her years.

When was it she had started to remember what had happened that day? It was years until her memory had fully come back. For a long time, she wasn't sure what was fact or what was part of her imagination, or a result of bad nightmares. It had taken months to get over the initial shock of waking up in the hospital following the accident. The injuries she had sustained healed over time but the loss of her memory and the trauma was the biggest problem. It was when the nightmares that Carol had been having had gotten worse and more frequent, that Bill had insisted that she see a doctor. Sleeping tablets didn't prevent the dreams and anxiety. She would still wake with sweat pouring down her back, tangled in sticky bedsheets. No amount of tablets could ever make things better. The grief, she couldn't share. The guilt inside her. Such guilt, day after day, eating away at her like a disease. Some days she had managed to push it all away to the back of her mind but it was never far from the surface. She had been unable to find the strength to undo what had already been done; it was too late. Some things were too hard to contemplate. So, she went on from day to day, weighed down by a secret which ate away at her, year after year.

The light of the day started to fade into late afternoon but Carol was unable to sleep so she just lay there, staring up at the ceiling, trying to block out her thoughts. She was so very tired.

CHAPTER 21

Sophie

Devon
Aug 1996

T HE MEAL HAD certainly been worth waiting for; no one had left a thing on their plates.

'That was absolutely marvellous Brenda. That was the best homemade pub grub I have ever had. You are a very lucky man, Jon.'

Sophie looked across the table to where Stevie was rubbing his stomach in appreciation of the meal he'd just finished devouring, before turning her attention back to Jon.

'I certainly am but then, she is a lucky lady, so I'm told.'

'Oh you,' Brenda giggled and nudged Jon in the ribs. 'Unfortunately, Jon enjoys the home cooking a little too much, if you get my drift. Don't you, my darling?'

'All the more of me to love, my dear,' Jon smiled affectionately at Brenda.

Sophie looked at the couple and thought how lovely they both were. Jon was really a giant of a man, easily about six foot four, or five. He'd once probably had a good head of hair. Now there were large tufts of white around the sides and back only. A long thin wave of white hair was combed over the top from the left side. He had large round blue eyes, which were heavily hooded but twinkled with what Sophie thought was rather wicked humour. He belly laughed and smiled a lot. His large full lips revealed a mouth full of his own teeth - a little worn with age but still all his own. He was quite a larger than life character. Not just did he carry a little too much weight around his middle for his long slender legs, but he had a large personality to match. He spoke very much as if he was still part of the squadron he had been recruited in to for so much of his earlier life. Even after leaving the R.A.F he had held down an important job as an air traffic controller, up until he retired early due to ill health. When Jon came into a room, his very presence commanded attention and respect. He was charming and formidable, but an absolute sweetie.

Brenda was, in comparison, a small woman, and very much the lady. Brenda only came up to Jon's shoulders and his stature seemed to dwarf her. Not her personality though. Brenda was as much fun and her own person as Jon was. She could keep you as well entertained as her husband could with tales of her life and what she had got up to. When Sophie last visited, Brenda had kept her captivated with the stories of how she and Jon had first met.

It had been very romantic; they had met at a dance, as many couples from that era did. Brenda had been in an awful lot of trouble that first evening they had met, as she had lost track of the time and had gotten in an hour later than her curfew. She had tried to sneak in quietly but was caught halfway up the stairs. She had been something of a rebel and even though she had been forbidden to see him again, she snuck out of her window the second time he was leave to meet with him, which had landed her in even more trouble. This did not deter Brenda and eventually her father gave up trying to keep her away from the airman. She and Jon were married on his fifth leave home. They had only known each other a matter of weeks and yet here they were, all these years later.

Brenda was an attractive woman, with cool blue eyes. She was in her seventies now and still wore her greying hair in a shoulder length bob. There were a few blond highlights running through it; she wore it very well. Her nature was gentle but firm and she was a sucker for any young children that came through the doors of the pub. Brenda always managed to find chocolate ice cream for them, even though it was not on the pub menu and it was never added to the patron's bill.

Sophie believed they had one son who had married a little later in life. He had no children of his own, only a stepdaughter. The older couple had missed out on much of her childhood, not having seen her in years. In fact, they had only met her twice and that was when she had been a moody teenager of thirteen or fourteen. The difficulty was with the son's job, they had explained to her once; he rarely got enough time off work for visits of any great length.

Feeling extremely full and a little sleepy, Sophie stretched and yawned.

'Don't know about anyone else but I could do with a lie down.'

'You are such a light weight, sweet cheeks. I do hope you're not going to be boring this holiday and spend half your time sleeping.' Stevie crossed his arms across his chest and pretended to be cross and pout.

'You are unbelievable Stevie Connors. You spent the whole journey snoring your head off, while I drove, and you have the cheek to say that to me.'

They all laughed and got up to make their way out. She planted a kiss on the cheek of both Jon and Brenda and could not help but grin when she saw Stevie do the same. Jon looked quite shocked for a moment and then grabbed Stevie's hand and gave him a firm handshake, muttering, 'Jolly pleased to meet you, young man,' in his most manly voice.

'Oh... and before we forget, our lovely son is honouring us with a visit,' Brenda exclaimed. 'I know he's a good bit older than you, young things, but it would be lovely if you came for dinner with us one evening this week. I'm sure he would love the company of you youngsters as well as us oldies. It would be much more fun. He's bringing his wife and to be honest, as I've told you before Sophie, we haven't met her more than a couple of times. I suppose it is a bit cowardly but the more of us there are, the easier the conversations will flow.'

'We'd be delighted to. I have heard such a lot about your son; it would be lovely to meet him at long last.' Sophie turned to Stevie and said, 'that would be lovely, wouldn't it, Stevie?'

'Absolutely. Any time spent in a pub with good food, wine and company, is a winner for me.'

Jane and Joe got in the front of the car and Sophie and Stevie got in the back. They started their drive back to Sand Banks feeling full and happy.

'I'm so pleased their son is making the effort to visit. They don't say as much, but I know that they miss him. He always tends to make work excuses and I know Brenda misses the contact a great deal more than she lets on,' Jane said.

'Well, we will just have to do our bit and help make sure his visit is pleasurable, so he visits more often Granny.'

Sophie was quiet for a moment then spoke again to her grandmother.

'Do you feel that way with Mum, Granny? You don't see a great deal of her, do you?'

There was an uncomfortable silence in the car.

'That's quite different darling. Your mother knows I love her. I've told her often enough but she seems to like her own company. I did ask her to come down here only the other week for a visit, but she told me she couldn't face the journey. It's difficult to know what to say to her. Your mother has always been a very self-sufficient young woman, who does things her own way in her own time. She knows where we are.'

Sophie felt that this was not entirely true but it was difficult to understand how she could bring her mother and grandmother closer together. They just seemed to misinterpret each other. Sophie knew they both loved each other, but somehow, they just didn't seem to give that impression.

The rest of the journey was done in relative silence and Sophie couldn't help but feel that she may have hit on a raw nerve with her gran. The sun lit up the whitewashed cottages in the village as they drove through; it looked like a scene from a chocolate box. The warm breeze, blowing through the windows, which were down, was filled with the aromas of freshly cut grass and salty sea air. They were greeted by Eddie as they drew up to the front porch. Jane had barely managed to get out of the car door, when he jumped up and planted both paws on her shoulders, nearly knocking her off her feet. His wet tongue flopped out, planting saliva all over her face.

'Get down you bad dog! You'll have me over.'

Eddie, dutifully, got down and his whole body moved from side to side as he practically wagged his tale off.

'In you come now, darlings. Why don't you both go and unpack your things and Sophie, you lie down for half an hour and re-charge your batteries. Stevie, if you don't want to rest, you can have a walk in the grounds or help Joe in the garden. He still has one or two things to do yet.'

'Well actually dear, I'm feeling a little weary after all that delightful food. Think I'll finish off the gardening tomorrow and catch forty winks myself.' Joe headed out to the garden to his favourite old deck chair to doze.

'Think I will have a quick lie down myself must be the sea air and food,' Stevie said and turned to follow the ladies.

Jane gave Sophie a conspiratorial wink as she made her way to the reception for their keys. Eddie was hot on her heels. Having been given the room numbers they would be staying in by Jane, Sophie and Steve headed up the staircase with their bags to their respective rooms to unpack. Joe headed off for a snooze on the patio.

Sophie lay on her bed. A breeze blew in through the window. The seagulls were making their usual noise but it was a sound that she loved. It meant holidays and fun and she must have drifted off. The next thing she was aware of was a knock at the door.

'Yoo-hoo, yoo-hoo. Are you awake, sweet cheeks? Can I come in?'

'Enter, oh pain in the butt.'

Sophie sat up and blinked herself awake. Stevie came in and jumped onto the bed next to her and lay back on the pillow.

'Have I been asleep long?' She asked.

'About an hour, I couldn't sleep myself. Isn't it divine here? I wish Jason could see how wonderful it is, so romantic.'

'Well, sorry about that. You'll just have to make do with me,' she smiled.

'Well, if I must. Now, are you ready to take me for a walk? I'm dying to see the beach and I want to take some picis of the sunset for Jason.'

'Let me splash some water on my face first. You get your camera, Romeo, and I'll meet you in the hallway downstairs in a minute.'

The weekend went past in relative peace. There were no moans of being bored from Stevie. Sophie certainly was seeing a different side to him. He did, indeed, seem to enjoy the peacefulness of Sand Banks. They went on several walks, taking Eddie with them. Eddie took to Stevie immediately, throwing himself at him at every opportunity. The peace and quiet was doing them both good and they were looking forward to dinner at the Rope and Anchor. Jon and Brenda's son had arrived with no last minute hitches, according to her gran.

They were returning from one of their many walks. Rain had been threatening to come in the last hour. The sky had been reasonably blue and clear when they had set out but, as was common on the coast, clouds soon blew in. The sky turned to a dark grey and the heavens opened, forcing them to take cover under the canopy of a large Oak tree. The sound of the rain beating down on the leaves overhead was thrilling.

'I love the sound of rain, especially when you are in a tent. Being under trees like this is even better. We stay dry but you feel at one with nature and its elements. The smell of the damp earth, the wet grass and sea air. It's fabulous, don't you think?' Stevie said as his eyes lit up with excitement.

'You really have surprised me the last few days, Stevie. I would never have put you down as the outdoors type but you seem to love it.'

Sophie was grinning up at him.

'There are many sides to me that people are unaware of. Just because I can be a loud party animal, does not mean that I don't enjoy the rugged outdoors as well. Most of my holidays growing up were spent camping or caravanning. My parents were very straight and predictable. Every summer holiday, out came the camping gear. They took us all over the place - never the same location twice and always with a visit to the odd stately home or museum along the way. Mum and Dad said that there was a whole load of places of interest to visit and they did their best to introduce me and my sister to most of them, let me tell you. As a youngster it seemed a little dull but now I'm rather glad they did drag us around the countryside; it was quite an education. They always had some little nugget of wisdom and interest to share about the places they took us to. They must have spent hours researching. The first time I ever experienced a fun fair was as a teenager with a friend's parent. With my own, the closest thing to a thrill, was a ride on a donkey on Southport sands, followed by a long walk through a forest, looking for red squirrels.'

With the word squirrel having been mentioned, Eddie's ears pricked up and he started to bark and wag his tail furiously. He started to rush around sniffing it out.

'At least you had a sister to share things with. Being an only sibling was pretty boring on holidays with my folks. We did sometimes go to fun fairs. I felt like a bit of a numpty going on rides on my lonesome, though, and it was embarrassing when Dad offered to come on a ride with me. Anyway, it looks like it is easing off a little. Let's head back.'

They started back to the B&B, with Eddie running from tree to tree in search of the elusive squirrel.

CHAPTER 22

Sophie

Devon
Aug 1996

THEY WERE DUE at the pub for dinner at seven o'clock sharp to meet the, often absent, son, who Jane was intrigued to meet. Jon was a stickler for time. Dinner at seven would mean exactly on the dot of seven. They arrived in plenty of time.

'There you are, excellent. Time for a small glass of something, before dinner. Let me introduce you to my son and his wife.'

Jon led the group through to a small room located just off to the left of the bar area. It could hold up to about sixteen people, at a squeeze, but there was ample room for just the eight of them dining there tonight. Two oblong tables had been pushed together and had been beautifully laden by Brenda. Stood by the window, looking at the view beyond, was Jon's son and his wife.

'Ewan, Ann, these are the friends we told you about. Joe, Jane, this is my son Ewan and his charming wife, Ann.'

Ewan extended his hand and shook Joe's, then he took Jane's, smiling warmly at her.

'Pleased to meet you both. Mum and Dad have spoken about you both so much I feel like we already know each other, isn't that right, Ann?' Jane smiled back.

'I know exactly what you mean. This is my granddaughter, Sophie, and her good friend, Stevie. They've been staying with us for a few days.'

Jane moved slightly to one side to let Sophie and Stevie move forward to shake their hands.

'Hi there, pleased to meet you. Unfortunately, we're back off to Manchester tomorrow but we've had a lovely few days, haven't we, Stevie?'

'We most certainly have. This place is just fab-u-lous... and I must say, Ewan, your mother is a divine cook,' Stevie exaggerated and drew out the word 'fabulous'.

Ann had moved forward to shake the young couple's hands but still had hold of Sophie's during the exchange. She hadn't said much at all; she seemed entranced by Sophie. Suddenly aware that she had been staring and hanging on to her, she blushed letting go.

'I'm so sorry. Please excuse my staring but you have a striking resemblance to my daughter, Ailsa, doesn't she, Ewan?'

'Now you mention it, I can see what you mean,' he replied, smiling at Sophie.

'Well,' Jane declared, 'you are very lucky if your daughter is a lovely as our Sophie! Now then, can I have a gin and tonic please, Jon? I am simply parched.'

'I'll come through and give you a hand,' Joe offered, following Jon through to the bar.

Soon, their group all had drinks and were sat down tucking into their dinner. During dinner, Stevie regaled them all with the story of him having 'come out '. He was keeping them all entertained in between Sophie digging him in the side occasionally, if she felt he was becoming too shocking. Everybody was in fits of laughter about his antics. It had all started with a question from Jane, who was always blunt.

'How did your parents react when they found out that you were interested more in boys than girls, Stevie?' Jane asked.

'Gran, that's a little personal,' Sophie admonished.

'It's fine, sweet cheeks,' Stevie reassured her. 'It was all rather a shock more so for me really. I'd brought a 'special friend' home with me from college one weekend. I thought that my folks were out. My friend, back then, had a thing for trying on women's clothes. So whenever he got the chance, off he would go and delve into any room that may offer the hope of feminine apparel. It didn't bother him whether or not this may be welcomed by the owners. He would just go right ahead. Well, there he was, with one of my mother's dresses on, her red lipstick plastered across his lips and he was parading around my room, doing his camp catwalk, when my mother knocked on the door. She walked straight in without waiting for a response. Neither of us had expected her home. I don't know who was more shocked: my friend, me, or mother. Poor Mum, she just stood there, her mouth moving open and closed like a goldfish in bowl. Then, out of the blue, she turned from my friend to me and said *sweetheart, I'm not sure that shade of blue dress really does your friend justice!'*

The whole table fell about with laughter.

'I couldn't believe that she had actually said that! Then, as if that wasn't enough, she goes into her bedroom, gets out another dress in a different colour from her wardrobe and brings it in for him to try on. Calmly, she then turns to me and says *Stevie, I think your father and I need to have a little chat with you.* Cool as a cucumber, just like that! Well, suffice it to say that I told them that I preferred boys to girls. I wasn't in the habit of cross dressing like my friend, so they didn't need to be concerned on that score. They weren't the least bit fazed. In fact, Mother appeared to be rather disappointed I wasn't a cross dresser, to be honest.'

At this stage in the story the occupants around the table were half under it. Tears were running down Sophie's cheeks. This was so typical of Stevie; he just carried on chatting away in a mock serious voice.

'Mother told me they had an inkling that I was possibly that way inclined, so were not hugely shocked. I really cannot understand how they could have guessed.'

Stevie did a theatrical sweep of his arms with this last statement, sending everybody into fresh roars of laughter.

The evening was, altogether, a huge success for Jon and Brenda. Their son and wife looked to be so at ease, happily seeming to enjoy the company. Sophie smiled to herself. To think that she thought Stevie could ever be bored was ridiculous, looking back. As long as Stevie had an audience, he was in his element. It didn't matter if it was only a handful of people; he would still entertain them. Stevie was just what the doctor ordered, she thought. It had been a lovely few days.

CHAPTER 23

Carol

Leeds
1996

THEY MIGHT BE able to shrink it with treatment but there were no promises. They could certainly manage her pain. A tumour in her brain. It was in a tricky area. Not in a place that was operable.

Cancer, tumour, inoperable. Three words. The only three words that were on a continual loop in her head. The oncologist was being very gentle, whilst being factual, when he talked to Carol about the scan. The diagnosis. The results. The treatment options. She couldn't take everything in. It didn't feel real. It was as if they were talking about someone else, not her. She'd sat there, frozen to the spot, unable to move, whilst they explained everything to her.

'Take some time to talk with your family. We'll see you again in three days' time. It's a lot to take in, we know,'

Do you though? Do you really know? Is it your brain? Carol thought.

What had she expected anyway? When she had been referred to the specialist following the scan, should she have realised then, maybe? No, she hadn't, or maybe looking back, she didn't want to accept the possibility they had found something.

There was no way of hiding things from Bill anymore, not now. She hadn't told him she'd first been for a scan – she didn't want to burden him. After years of headaches, even she was sick of hearing herself moan. She'd presumed he would be sick of it all as well. So she hadn't told him. Now, here she was, leaving the hospital, unsure of where she was even going. She walked around aimlessly, eventually picking up a taxi.

The taxi pulled up outside their home. She'd been uneasy about driving today.

The symptoms had gotten worse. It wasn't just the constant headaches, dizziness and sickness, there was also a numbness that came and went in her arm so she felt unable to trust herself in the car.

When Bill was home, she would have to sit him down and talk to him. Why hadn't she told him what was going on sooner? It had been idiotic, in retrospect. Somehow, if she didn't talk about it, she felt that it wasn't that serious. It would all be alright! Boy, how wrong had she been.

She sat silently, waiting for Bill to get home, reflecting on the day. She had been feeling ghastly. Her appointment was early so she had to leave before Bill. She had to make an excuse as to why she had to be up and out and why she was getting a taxi and not driving. *She was just going back to the G.P. as her head was particularly severe today*, she had told him. He had wanted to drop her off. She had made him go to work and told him not to fuss. How very stupid she'd been! It wasn't just Bill that had to be told, but Sophie too. Dear god, how was she going to find the strength?

She made her way to the kitchen to make herself a cup of tea whilst she waited, trying to take her mind off of it. She was terrified. She was going to die. She didn't want to. She just wasn't ready to leave Bill and Sophie behind. *It isn't fair. Why me? Because I did a bad thing. I was selfish. I should've done something when I knew. I've lived a lie. It's a punishment. Lies always have a way of catching up and I'm being punished.* She was going to be sick. She staggered towards the kitchen sink. Holding on to the edge of it for support, she leaned over and threw up. She heaved and heaved, until there was nothing in her stomach. The acidic bile came up into her nose, leaving her throat burning and her nose running. She wiped the back of her hand angrily across her mouth.

Automatically, she ran the tap to clean the mess from the sink. She turned herself around, staring out towards the table, her eyes glazed over. Her legs gave way again and she slipped to the floor, as she wailed in despair. She cried and cried whilst snot ran down her face. She couldn't stop the endless tears coming. Rocking herself back and forth, she gripped her arms around her knees. Her body remained balled up, as she wept and wept. Until eventually, she was spent. Exhausted, she pulled herself up and slowly walked over to the kitchen chair, flopping down into it heavily. Her whole body and head felt like a lead weight. She couldn't move. She sat there, staring, seeing nothing, feeling nothing. Empty.

It was hours later when Bill found her, still sitting there, in the dark, with her coat on.

'What are you doing sat there with your coat on? What on earth's the matter?'

Bill, turning the light on and taking in the sight of Carol for the first time, was panicked. He knew that something was wrong.

'Carol, Carol, what is it? What's upset you? Is Sophie okay?'

'Sophie's fine. Bill...oh Bill, I'm so sorry!'

She couldn't bear to look at him. She just covered her face with her hands. He barely caught her words.

'I should have told you sooner but it seemed unnecessary and I was wrong and now it's such a shock,' she blurted out, hardly stopping for breath. Her words were barely distinguishable from one another. 'I don't know where to start.'

He quietly went to the table and sat in the chair next to her, taking her hands in his. They were like ice. He cupped her chin, forcing her face towards him, gently, his eyes meeting hers.

Calmly and pragmatically, Bill said, 'I suggest you start at the beginning and we can take it from there.'

This was so typical of Bill, always cool and reassuring. When she met his eyes, she was unable to hide from him the anguish that she felt.

'I had this appointment today with a specialist at the hospital. I've had some investigations done.'

'I thought you had an appointment with the G.P today?'

'I saw the G.P. a few weeks ago, about the headaches and he wanted the hospital to do a scan. Investigate them further. It wasn't just the headaches he was concerned about. I've been feeling wretched for weeks. Dizziness, sickness, numbness in my arm.'

'What? Why haven't you told me any of this?'

'I don't know,' Carol struggled to find the right words, 'I don't know what to say. I should have but I didn't. I'm sorry.' She paused, mentally preparing herself for his reaction to the next bit. 'I went for the scan results, the bloods etc. and it's not good, Bill.' She allowed him to digest this information.

His eyes searched her face for more but she felt unable to go on.

'What did the specialist say, Carol?'

There was a silence where all she could do was look at him, feeling completely helpless, unable to go on and say the words which she knew would tear him apart.

'Carol, what did he say?' He repeated his words with care, not taking his eyes from her face.

'There is no easy way to say it...They've found a tumour.'

'A tumour,' he repeated.

'Yes. A tumour. Cancer. They can't operate. It is what they call *inoperable* because of where it is,' she said.

Once the words had spilt out of her mouth, they hung in the air like poisonous gas trapped in the room with them. No escape. No way out. She felt like she was suffocating. He never took his eyes away from hers. She could feel his hands squeezing her own, holding onto her as if she would disappear if he let go. It was some moments until he found his voice.

'Of course they will be able to operate. Why on earth not?'

She snapped at him, 'what do you suppose inoperable means, Bill? I've just said, because it's in an awkward place to get to. Attached to some major veins in my brain, or something. I can't remember. They can only manage it with medication. They can't guarantee anything.'

'That's ridiculous. You've only had a few headaches. How can they be so sure? Who did you see? What sort of tumor? I want to talk to this specialist myself.' He barked the questions in a flash of anger, raising his voice.

She looked back at him, matching his anger.

'You can talk to him as much as you like. It isn't going to change the diagnosis. They gave me another appointment to go back in and talk some more. They'll want to discuss a treatment program. I wanted to talk to you. I think you need to be with me next time.'

'I should damn well think you did want to talk to me. Why didn't you tell me you were seeing a specialist? For god's sake Carol, didn't you think I had a right to know? I'm your husband.'

He looked angry and wild, like a wounded animal that had been cornered; he had tears rolling down his cheeks.

'I'm sorry. I'm so sorry,' Carol could feel the tears start to well up in her again, 'I should have told you. Please don't be angry,' she started to get hysterical, 'I don't know what to do Bill. I'm scared, so scared!'

He suddenly looked utterly deflated, like a balloon having had the air let out of it. His face crumpled and he looked like he had aged ten years in the last five minutes. He pulled her to him. Holding her firmly in his arms, calming her down.

'No, no, don't be sorry. I'm sorry you've had to deal with it on your own, that you couldn't tell me. I didn't mean to rage at you, love. It's just such a shock. I love you so much. I just can't take it in. I can't bear the thought of losing you. I'm being selfish.'

Bill rocked her gently, trying to sooth her as best he could. They both kept hold of each other, tightly. They were both silently weeping and unable to let go of one another.

'It's going to be alright, love. I've got you now. You really should have told me. Honey. Why on earth did you keep this from me? I should have been with you today.'

'I know, I know. I kept thinking it would be nothing more than stress. I've had headaches on and off over the years. I just thought that the other things were part and parcel of hormones or something. I should have told you. I am so sorry.'

'Shhh. Shhh, now. It's fine. We can deal with this together now.'

He continued to rock her. She was happy for him to just keep holding her and never wanted him to let her go.

It seemed like hours had passed as they both sat in the kitchen. They didn't speak. Neither one knew what to say to the other. Time seemed to stand still. Eventually, when they were both exhausted and emotionally drained, they pulled apart. She got slowly to her feet and got them both some tissues from the kitchen drawer to wipe their faces.

'What now?' He said in a hoarse whisper.

Now it was Carol's turn to be the strong one, for him.

'Now, we have a cup of tea and I will tell you in detail, as much as I took in. Then, when we go and see the oncologist for my next appointment, you will know as much as I do.'

CHAPTER 24

Ailsa

Manchester
Sept 1996

THE EXHIBITION HAD gone well. Ailsa and Max had enjoyed a nice, cold bottle of sparkling cava to celebrate. Max had been full of it. He had managed to get two commissions from the exhibition, which was great and they promised to bring in at least two thousand a piece. He would be spending a lot of hours in the Studio over the next few weeks and then he would be putting together his ideas for the next exhibition, which Ailsa was dreading him doing with the 'incredible Christine'.

The next morning, they both woke up late. They didn't have any firm plans as it was Sunday. They were both rather shattered with all the last-minute running around the last couple of days, so neither of them felt any guilt at waking after ten thirty.

'Coffee, oh master?' asked Ailsa as she rolled over and stroked Max's cheek which was sporting two day's stubble.

'Um, yeah, lovely. Make mine two spoons of coffee. I want to do a bit of research later and need the caffeine kick.'

She slipped out from under the warm duvet, grabbing her old toweling bathrobe, which had seen better days. In bare feet, she padded through to the kitchen area and flicked the switch on the kettle. She grabbed two dirty mugs from the sink and washed them, ready for the coffee. It was quite ridiculous that they only had two mugs. Mental note to self - buy some more mugs. She trotted back to bed with two steaming cups, passing the stronger one to Max.

As they were enjoying the last of their coffee, the phone rang. Max reached for it and a large grin crossed his face as he heard who it was.

"Hello to you, too! Really... yes... not a bad idea... yeah... ok... I'll give the matter some thought... umm… yeah definitely be dramatic... I think we would have to go big but simple lines... could use some of the rails but I will have to try and source the... hey and thanks for suggesting me to the council, that's great… no, really that is totally awesome, Chrissie.'

Max had a beaming smile on his face as he placed the phone back on the receiver.

'Guess who that was and what I've been offered?' Max asked, still beaming.

Inwardly rolling her eyes, Ailsa replied, 'I would hazard a guess at Christine Hancock? And I wouldn't dare to guess what she has offered?' She couldn't keep the annoyance or sarcasm from her voice, as much as she knew she shouldn't have reacted this way.

'Nice, Ailsa. Nice. Can't you just try to be supportive? Just for once. Would it kill you?'

'Sorry! What did Chrissie want?'

'If you must know, some guy in London, that Christine knows, has a friend on the council in Leeds and they are looking for an up and coming sculptor to do a memorial piece to commemorate the Leeds rail disaster nearly 25 years ago. The money won't be great but it's a huge honor to be put forward.'

Ailsa went cold.

'The derailment in seventy- two?' She whispered.

'Yes. Isn't that great?'

'No... I mean yes… it is an honor but... well, not great for the victims and their families.'

'It's great, bloody great - there's going to be a memorial dedicated to the victims,' he pauses, noticing Ailsa's face for the first time. 'Christ Ailsa, you've gone as white as a sheet. What's the matter?'

'Sorry, I, um, I was just taken by surprise. It's just that my baby sister was on that train, Max. It's a bit of a shock, that's all. It was just such a long time ago and it's not something I've thought about for a while.'

'God, hon. I had no idea. You've never mentioned it. I mean, I know you had a kid sister that had died young but I had no idea. Jesus, Ailsa. Were you and your parents involved in the accident as well?'

'No, it's really complicated. Mum, Dad and I weren't on the train at the time. It was, frankly, an awful time for my parents. My sister was snatched from her pram some hours before. A woman in the village took her. She was apparently suffering some sort of depression after losing her own child from cot death. It seems she had changed trains and ended up on the one that de-railed, god knows where she was heading to. They never found out why she had travelled from Scotland all the way down there. The woman and my sister were both probably killed outright, according to the coroner. I was pretty much unaware, being so young. I'm sad to say I don't really remember anything about her.'

'It must have been really rough on your parents, though. God, what a nightmare for them.'

'Yeah, well, it was. My dad, from what I can gather, drowned his sorrows in the bottle and he moved out when I was still young. My mum though, well, I don't think she's ever recovered from it. She is good at hiding things, my mum. She always tries to be up-beat but…I caught her a couple of times going through my sister's things. There is a sadness in her face sometimes but if she catches me looking at her, she will brush it away. I suppose you never get over losing a child.'

'No, I don't suppose you do. Surely it will be nice for the families, though? Some way of acknowledging what happened, I mean.'

'I suppose… but it will also unearth a lot of memories for the survivors and those people who lost loved ones. It's such a long time ago now. Maybe it should have been done years ago.'

'True, it should. Then again, maybe it would have been too raw. You know how bureaucracy works. The council has probably got extra funds they need to get rid of before the end of the financial year. I know it sounds cold and cynical but it's usually the case.'

'Maybe. Who knows? I'll need to let my mum know, warn her. It will bring back some painful stuff for her. Look, do you mind if I get out for some fresh air. I just need some time on my own, hon.'

'No, don't be daft. Course I don't mind.'

Ailsa felt strangely disturbed by the past being brought up. She needed to get out of the flat to clear her head. Her emotions had taken her by surprise. She wouldn't have thought that a reminder of her family's loss would have made her feel quite this bad. A good walk would do her good and give her time to gather her thoughts. She would need to have a conversation with her mum; she didn't want her blind-sided by this.

CHAPTER 25

Sophie

Manchester
Sept 1996

SOPHIE AWOKE TO the phone on her bedside table ringing. At first, she thought that it was her alarm and then she realized that it was Sunday morning and there was no work today. Relief washed over her but then annoyance took over as she realised that it was only 9.30am. Who on earth would be calling at this time on a Sunday morning? Sophie pressed the button on her mobile to answer the call.

'Hello'

She could not make out the number; her eyes were still adjusting to the light.

'Hello, love. It's your dad. Hope I haven't woken you up.'

'Well, actually you have but don't worry. What makes you call so early on a Sunday morning? Is everything alright?'

'We just wanted to know if you have any plans today. Your mother and I fancied a trip out and thought we would bob over… if you're not busy.'

'Well, yes. I mean, no. I'm not busy. That would be lovely. What time will you get here? I will need to get some shopping in if you want to eat, or we can go out for lunch?'

'We reckon that we would get to you around 12.30 but don't go to any trouble. We are just as happy with a sandwich and a cup of tea. Not sure your mum's up to any noisy pub for lunch. Just be good to see you.'

'Right, no problem. I'll expect you around 12.30ish then. Bye, Dad.'

'Bye, love. See you then.'

Sophie looked at the phone, a little puzzled. It was very out of character for her parents to just pop over on the spur of the moment. They had never done that before. Her mother hated any journey that took longer than twenty minutes and whenever they had visited before, it was always planned well in advance.

Sophie got up and jumped in the shower to wake her up some more. It promised to be a nice day from what little she had glimpsed, so she decided to walk down to the deli on the high street for some bits for lunch. Her dad loved the stuffed olives from there and her mum liked their homemade quiche. Plus, the exercise would do her good. But first, she would have a cup of tea.

As Sophie walked briskly down Park Road to the High Street, she took in how busy the local park was. There were several dads with young children on bikes and scooters. Dad's day, she thought and wondered, not for the first time, if she would ever meet someone special enough to have children with. It was chilly but fresh and the sun showed the leaves on the trees which were starting to turn red and burnished copper with the onset of autumn. It was a glorious day, even if a little on the chilly side. It was a lovely park - very quaint and surrounded with Victorian houses on all four sides. It even had a friendly society, set up by the locals to organize various events throughout the year. It was full of beautiful trees with dozens of rhododendron bushes lining the green railings. There was a bowling green, a tennis court and a small children's play area, as well as a nature walk in a small corner off to the right. In addition to the various families out today, there were dog walkers taking their Sunday strolls.

The deli was only a ten- minute walk from where her flat was. She had often enjoyed a late breakfast there, reading the Sunday paper. As she went to push open the deli door, she was still thinking about the strange phone call from her father. She was so lost in her own thoughts that she hadn't noticed the young woman approaching from the other side of the doorway and the woman had to jump back quickly to avoid being hit.

'God, I'm so sorry! Nearly took you out there. I'm in a world of my own.'

She met the other woman's eyes and she had the weirdest feeling. The woman looked directly back at her and had a shocked expression on her face.

'No problem,' the woman muttered, as she quickly moved around her and went out to the street. She continued to glance around at her as she went. Sophie was still stood holding the door open, staring after her. She thought she knew her but couldn't quite place where from. The young woman disappeared around the next corner so she could no longer see her. Strange. It was as if the woman had known her too. She let the matter drift from her mind as she was still puzzling over her parent's visit. She turned her attention to the deli counter, no longer distracted by the young woman she had almost collided with.

She left with three slices of the homemade quiche, a large tub of coleslaw, a small bag of new potatoes and a bag of mixed salad. On the way home, her mind drifted back to her encounter in the Deli. It had been the eyes. They were an almost perfect reflection of her own, she thought. It was uncanny. Their hair had been slightly different; her own was quite curly and unruly, whereas the woman's had been straight and cut into a neat shoulder length bob.

When she got home, she turned her mind to her parents visit. The flat was already quite tidy. When she was living alone, it was easy to keep it that way; she had an organized nature. However, the bathroom needed freshening up and clean towels putting out. The buzzer to her flat sounded almost at the exact time they said they would arrive - 12.30. Sophie smiled to herself; Dad was so organized, always on time, never late, never too early. Sophie buzzed them up.

'Hi, it's so great to see you both. It seems like ages. What a great idea coming over like this.'

Sophie threw her arms around her mum first, and then her dad.

'No traffic on the road so it didn't take too long. How are you, love? You look well.'

'I am, Dad. How are you two?'

'Not so bad. Not so bad,' replied her mother.

She didn't actually look that great though. Sophie thought her mother had lost weight and she looked grey and pasty.

'I've been to the deli and got us some quiche for lunch. I meant to get you some olives, Dad, but it completely slipped my mind when I was in there. Why don't you both sit on the sofa and I'll make us some coffee.'

'Oh sweetheart, just some tea for me, if you don't mind. I've gone off coffee,' her mother said.

Sophie went to make some drinks whilst her father prowled around the room. He seemed agitated and her mother kept looking up at him. They were both unusually quiet.

'O.K you two, I know something's not right. Dad you are prowling like a panther and Mum you are clenching and unclenching your hands. The last time you were both like this, it was to tell me I couldn't go on the school trip to Paris. Come on, spill the beans.'

'This isn't easy,' her father said. 'Come and sit down, sweetheart. We need to talk to you.'

Sophie sat down next to her mum. Her mother took her hand but wouldn't look at her.

'Mum, what is it? You and Dad aren't splitting up, are you?'

'No, nothing like that. Nothing like that, at all.'

Her father sat down on the other side of Sophie. Her father took her other hand.

'Your mum has not been well lately, with her headaches getting worse. The G.P. sent her for some tests and they revealed that there is a tumor.'

Her mum almost flinched as he said this.

Sophie felt as if she had been hit by a sledgehammer; she had not been expecting anything like that.

'I presume they are going to treat it, Mum?'

Sophie turned to her mother but her mother would still not meet her eye. She did, however, reply.

'They are not able to operate. They can only manage it and its symptoms. The top and bottom of it is that they are giving me chemotherapy, which may give me longer.'

'Mum, no... Dad, that can't be right surely?'

Sophie turned her pleading eyes from one to the other.

'Sweetheart, I'm very much afraid that your mother is right. I can hardly take it in myself. We have spoken a great deal with the specialist and they hope to arrest the growth of the tumor with treatment but it is in a difficult place to remove. To even try to operate could leave your mother paralyzed. Even if they managed to operate without causing such damage, it would not get it all out. Operating just isn't an option.'

'When did you find out? Why are you only just telling me?' Sophie felt angry and upset.

'We were only told at the beginning of the week. We wanted to have all the facts before talking to you. We are hoping that the chemotherapy will help stop the growth but it is too early to know yet. Your mum only got the treatment program on Friday.'

'Mum, are you in any pain?' Her mother then looked at her. 'No darling. None whatsoever at this present time. Not now they have given me some stronger medication for the pain; it is quite bearable. I'm so sorry Sophie, my love. This is not the sort of thing you want to be telling your child but we had to let you know, to prepare you for when the worst happens.'

'Never mind with all that. It's not your fault, so why say sorry. That's stupid. The treatments for ca...,' she thought better of the using the C word. She just couldn't bring herself to say it. For it to be real. 'These treatments are marvelous these days. I can move back home and get a job locally and then I can help more.'

'It's called cancer and we will all have to get used to saying it, but there we are. You will most certainly not move back home. You have your own life to lead and your father and I can manage very well between us, thank you.'

'Oh Mum. Please don't be stubborn. I want to be with you.'

Sophie was crying now and Carol scooped her daughter up in her arms.

'I know you do, darling, and when the time is right, you can come home and help. Right now, your dad and I are perfectly fine. Visit as often as you like but please, for my sake, carry on with your own life for the time being.'

Carol felt a wave of relief that her daughter had been told. Her and Bill had argued about whether to tell her straight away or to wait. As it turned out, Bill had said that Sophie would be angry if they kept her in the dark about things and he had been right. Carol understood, too, that selfishly, it was a weight off her shoulders to have them both know. They could help each other through things. The next person they would have to tell would be her mother. Left up to Carol, she would have kept it from her for as long as possible but she was aware that she and Sophie had a special bond and Sophie would need to share her anxieties with her grandmother. At one time, Carol would have been jealous of that bond but now, she was utterly grateful for it.

CHAPTER 26

Ailsa

Manchester
Sept 1996

ILSA KEPT GLANCING around at the woman who had nearly knocked her flying. The woman had stayed in the doorway staring after her. That was so creepy. Ailsa wondered if the woman had been as surprised as she was. The likeness between them both was uncanny. It was the eyes that had really got to Ailsa. It was as though she knew the woman and could see inside her soul. Wow, that was really off the scale. It had taken her mind off her own anxieties. It was of no use. She was going to have to go back and speak to that woman; it was too uncanny. Ailsa, who had got almost halfway down the side road, turned around and started back towards the Deli. As she got to the corner she stopped. The woman would think she was a crack pot. What would she even say? *Hi, my names Ailsa, who are you? And why do we look so alike?* No,

Ailsa thought. She would definitely sound slightly deranged but she also couldn't walk away.

Ailsa could never walk away if something caught her interest. Her mother would often say: *That nose of yours will be your downfall one day.* By the time Ailsa had decided to go ahead and introduce her-self, she caught sight of the woman coming out of the Deli. The woman turned in the opposite direction to Ailsa and set off along the High Street. Ailsa decided to take a stroll in that direction. The woman turned left down Park Road, aptly named due to their being a small park situated on the left corner, near the bottom end of the road. Ailsa kept her distance, feeling a little bit like a stalker. Ailsa didn't have far to follow as the woman took a right turn just after the park. She turned into the driveway of the fifth house on the right. Ailsa kept back a little and waited for the woman to go in. It was too late now to approach her but she could not leave it there. Having followed her for ten minutes, she felt that she should try and go a bit further. Ailsa casually walked up to the driveway.

It was a Victorian house which had been split into flats. The front door looked to have three names next to three buttons. Ailsa took a sneaky look towards the windows and quickly ran to the front door. There were three names. Flat 1: John Adams, flat 2: Ahmena Ahmed and flat 3: Sophie Woods. Sophie…she was probably Sophie. Well, that was her best guess. What now? Should she buzz her? No, she would certainly appear to be a stalker then. No, she thought. It was best to leave, quit whilst she was ahead. Ailsa felt a bit silly when she really thought about it. It had been a difficult morning and she was overreacting. I mean it was possible she supposed they could be related. Ailsa could have cousins on her birth-dad's side of the family. She could check with her mum and see if she knew of any. Although she was sure that there was no contact with that side of the family.

Ailsa suddenly felt a real pang of being homesick. It was probably the shock of being reminded about the train crash. Ailsa hadn't thought about it for years; there was no reason to really. In all honesty, she hadn't missed someone she couldn't remember. There were times, though, that she had felt envious of friends who had siblings to share things with. It must have been so hard for her mum. Ailsa set off back towards her own flat. A trip home to see her mum was what she needed. As soon as she got in, she would give her a call and arrange a trip home.

PART 3

CHAPTER 27

Ailsa

Scotland
1996

ANN HURRIED TO answer the knock on the front door and was thrilled that Ailsa had arrived.

'It was certainly a lovely surprise to get a call from you saying you were on your way home. You must be shattered.'

Ann pulled her daughter into the lounge and in front of the roaring fire she had going.

'Come here, let me look at you. You're a sight for sore eyes. It's so good to see you; I can't tell you how much I've missed you.'

Ann went from hugging her daughter to pushing her away and looking at her.

'Why the visit now? Have you and Lord Max fallen out?'

The relationship between her daughter and Max had been a little tempestuous from the start, so Ann wasn't surprised to see her daughter.

Ailsa was shocked at the term her mother had used in relation to Max.

'Mum, what makes you call him that?' Ailsa said, laughing.

'Sorry, Ailsa but he is a little pompous, isn't he?'

'Full of his own importance too,' Ailsa said. 'How come you have him so sussed and I am only just getting the real him?'

'Old age and a beady eye,' Ann laughed. 'You may think your old mum is a bit behind the door because I'm not well travelled but I have a nose for people. It's always rosy in the beginning. I, more than anyone, know that, having lived with your father.'

'Well, you're bang on with your assessment of Max,' Ailsa said, wearily.

'Stop right there, get your coat off and sit down. I'll make us a nice cup of hot chocolate and you can tell me all about it before Ewan gets home. He's having to work late, otherwise he would have been here to welcome you home. He should only be an hour or so though. We can have a nice catch up on our own before he rolls in.'

Ann left Ailsa in the lounge in front of the lovely roaring fire. Ailsa looked around. It had been re-decorated since she had last been home. The walls were now a soft beige, except for the wall where the fireplace was, which was picked out in a mossy green. There were new curtains and cushions in a deep wine red, with small flecks of beige running through them. Although it was the same three- piece suite they had always had, the red and beige cushions on the brown worn leather sofa looked invitingly warmer than the cream cushions that used to be there.

'Here we are. Your favourite: hot chocolate and chocolate digestives. We can have our meal when Ewan gets home - cottage pie with cheddar mash.'

'Oh Mum, you're the best. All of my favourites.'

Ailsa felt her eyes sting with tears at the warmth and love she felt for this wonderful woman.

'Hey now, no tears. You'll set me off.'

'Sorry, I'm just tired.'

'No doubt due to Lord Max putting you through your paces, eh.'

Ailsa laughed again as her mother used the term in connection with Max.

'He just gets so caught up with what he wants. I feel like I come second to everything else going on in his life. He's working with this woman and I don't trust her at all.'

Ann had never been overly keen on Max but her daughter was impulsive, stubborn even. When she made her mind up to do something, there was no stopping her. It wasn't that she disliked him but he lacked the depth of emotion that Ann wanted in a partner for her daughter. He was a little shallow; he made the right noises but there was no depth to him.

'What makes you distrust her?'

'It's not just her...it's him too,' Ailsa whispered.

Ann was not too surprised to hear that Ailsa didn't trust this man. She hadn't herself. It had just been a gut feeling.

'He is so absorbed in his work, which is good for an artist, but he takes no interest in my work. We're supposed to be a team and he only seems to put himself forward for work. For example, back in August we were doing this exhibition. Mainly Max's sculptures and a couple of new unknown graduate's work. I did all the designs, from the printing of the programs, to the posters. I organized the personalized invites, the venue, and all the background stuff. The whole point wasn't just to help him, as he seemed to assume. It was about my career as well. I'm good at designing and have a flair for finding the right venues and putting stuff together to create the right platform for the exhibitions. We had invited people that could do us both good. Max, however, was the center of attention. Don't get me wrong, I expected it, but he could so easily have made the right introduction to the right people for me. He could have acknowledged my work: the brilliant girlfriend that had put the whole thing together, who was responsible for the advertising and the reason the venue was so packed out etc. I worked so hard to get it all flowing together and I may as well have been invisible. Now this Christine bloody Hancock has offered him work and I have a feeling that the last time they worked together something went on between them. I have no proof but, as much as I love him, I'm not blind. He has always been the confident flirty type but the relationship he has with this woman feels something more than just business.'

Ailsa, at last, stopped for breath and gave Ann a chance to respond.

'Ailsa, you're not a fool. There is a reason we call it a gut instinct. It's there to warn us to be careful. Yes, you love him and don't want to believe he could hurt you in that way. However, sometimes men are stupid, even the best of them. They are wired differently from us women. That doesn't mean to say that Max has cheated on you. It just means that your instincts may well be right about his connection with this woman. Have you asked him outright if there was anything between them?'

'I have and he has denied it, telling me that it is just the way she is, you know the sort, all boobs and flirtation, wants what she sees etc.'

'Do you believe him when you look him in the eye?'

'That's just it, I do. Then again, I don't. I just don't know…but I think that I more *don't believe him*, than I do. It's horrible.'

'Well, I can't advise you on that one, honey. The only thing I would say is keep a close eye on the situation. Lies have a way of coming out and biting people back, so if something has gone on, then the truth will out. There is no way to avoid getting hurt. At this stage, you are already emotionally invested. Just don't let him get away with cheating on you if you find out he has. Once a cheater, always a cheater. Don't accept any excuses because there's never one good enough. Sounds like you've given him the benefit of the doubt once, not again, though, for your own sake. In a relationship, there needs to be trust. No trust, no peace of mind.'

'Thanks, Mum. I needed to hear that. I'd already come to that conclusion. It's just so difficult when you are so close to someone. It confuses things. I just needed a break away from him for a couple of days to get my head straight.'

'I'm always here, honey. You know that.'

Ailsa paused, hesitant.

'There is another thing I needed to talk to you about,' she began. There was no easy way to say what she needed to, so Ailsa came right out with it. Like tearing a plaster off.

'Max has been put forward to do a sculpture as a memorial to the victims and the families of the train crash that Susan died in.'

Ann looked momentarily taken aback. The shock, visible on her face, was quickly replaced with a gentle smile.

'Honey, that is lovely news. It's a little late in the day but lovely all the same.'

'Really? That's how you feel? I was so worried it would dredge up painful memories?'

'The memories are always there, love. Maybe not as painful as the first few years but they're there all the same. Good days, bad days. I think a memorial is lovely, though. It's an acknowledgement that these people were ours and they were lost. In a strange way, it's a comfort. There may be some people that feel differently but I like the idea.'

She was so relieved that her mum felt that way. It felt good to be home. She needed to make more of an effort to spend time with her mum and dad. She'd been putting her relationship with Max before everything else that was important to her. It really wasn't healthy. It was time that she took more control over her emotions. She'd let her heart rule her head. Sometimes though, it's easier said than done.

CHAPTER 28

Carol

Leeds
Oct 1996

IT HAD BEEN a few weeks since she and Bill had told Sophie about the tumor. She was getting worse as she hadn't responded to the treatment as well as they had hoped and time was running out. There was a knot in her stomach every time she thought about what she had to do. The fear of losing the love of her family over the last few weeks of her life filled her with more dread than the illness and death itself. With the diagnosis, came the worry about some cancers being passed down through genetics. Should Sophie ever get any sort of chronic illness, there would be no history there. Any history they looked at would be wrong. Blood tests could even throw everything Bill thought into complete chaos. She wouldn't be around to provide the answers.

In the months following the accident, she'd been out of it. Her memories of the accident, after coming out of the coma, was like being under murky water. There were blurred pictures and sounds with no clear vision. It was Bill that had offered her bits of information surrounding her movements that day. Then she had come around in the hospital. The pain in her head was pounding and there was a whooshing roar that infiltrated her ears. There was an incredible sick feeling. The first few days she had drifted in and out of sleep until her body and mind had slowly started to recover. There were a lot of concerned faces around her those first few days and she'd receded into sleep where she felt safe. Her baby was safe and that was all that mattered.

The nightmares that had followed the accident had been terrifying. They were fragmented like a broken mirror - bits of memories all scattered and out of place. After she had been at home for a few weeks, they had started with a vengeance. The most terrifying one was where she was on the train, it was very crowded, and the guard was moving along the train's corridor, checking people's tickets. When he had reached where she was, he had lent down and smiled. *Ticket please.* She had looked up, feeling helpless. She couldn't find it in her purse. His mouth had turned into a snarl and his face had started to rot into a putrefied ghastly mask. *WHAT, NO TICKET?* He had roared down at her. His mouth was gaping and she could see rotten brown teeth with saliva running down the side of what was left of his mouth. A stink of faeces was emanating from him which made her feel sick. He had snatched Sophie from her arms before she had chance to react. *I WILL HAVE THIS THEN, INSTEAD. ALL FARES NEED TO BE PAID.* He turned away from her, pushing Sophie into a satchel that was over his shoulder and Sophie was disappearing into the bag which was getting bigger and bigger. She couldn't move; she was paralyzed with fear. The guard moved on down the train and the train got longer and longer, turning into a tunnel and the guard got smaller and smaller. She had been unable to move after him. It was as if she had a tight band of iron around her upper body, pinning her down. She was screaming. She had woken to find Bill holding both her arms and calling her name. He said it had frightened him to death. He had soothed her and held her in his arms and talked gently to her until she had calmed down.

The next morning, he'd suggested that she see the doctor, that the trauma of the accident had caused the nightmare. His explanation seemed to make sense and she didn't think much more about it until another nightmare a few nights later. The nightmares continued over the next few months and had taken different forms. All of them involved Sophie. Carol had been to the G.P. and he had prescribed a course of sleeping pills. In the day she was groggy. She had stopped taking them.

CHAPTER 29

Carol

Leeds
1977

'I CAN'T BELIEVE it's been at least five years since we last saw each other. I still think about that awful day. It seems like such a long time ago now. I am so sorry I didn't come and see you after the accident but there never seemed to be a right time. Poor Bill. He was in such a state when he called and told me about the accident. It must have been a nightmare for him to get a message out of the blue from the police. Poor guy, working away and getting a call like that. Up until I had spoken to him, he hadn't even known you and I had met up for lunch that day.'

Jenny had just given Carol one of her bear hugs and the two mums sat down.

'Don't be daft. There was a lot going on and I wasn't really up to visitors at the time. Life gets away from you and before you know it, you haven't caught up in the longest time. To be honest, I had no recollection that we had even met up that day either, and things are still a bit sketchy,' she smiled reassuringly at her friend. 'It is one of the reasons that I arranged to see you today, actually. I have gone over and over things in my head but, even now, all these years later, it is such a jumble. I guess, if I am honest, I have avoided you the last few years. It was just strange. It was almost like I couldn't go back to that time and you were part of such an awful day that I tried to erase you from my life, as well as the memory of the accident. Do you hate me for it?'

'Not at all. Friends are friends for life. I kind of got that you were avoiding me but it had to be up to you. I didn't want to push it, so whenever you were too busy when I called, I told myself you would be in touch when and if you could face me, and here you are. It is hardly surprising really; it must have been such a traumatic experience. Anyway, we had the funniest afternoon and never stopped laughing. Can you remember any of it?'

'Not really. That is why I suggested meeting up today, without the little-uns, so we could go through that day without interruption and see if you can fill in some of the blanks for me.'

'I will do my best. Do you remember that we met near the library to start with?'

'Yes, I vaguely remember that but then it all gets confused. I can remember that we had tea. We did some shopping, although I cannot remember in which order we did things. I remember chatting to another woman, about my age, about her baby. The baby was very unsettled; I was trying to reassure her but can't remember where we were.' Carol squinted, as if trying to focus on the memory.

'No, I don't remember that. It was just you and me all day. We spent most of it pretending that we were rather rich housewives, out spending our husband's bank balances. We were being rather giddy and silly. Do you remember going into that designer shop on the high street and us both trying on evening dresses and the snooty shop assistant? That was about the only woman we had any conversation with. There wasn't any baby there, only ours, and she kept frowning at them as if they were going to suddenly spontaneously combust. The woman was a fright and I'm afraid we were rather mean. The more she frowned, the more we had her running in and out of the stock room for things for us to try on. We thought she was going to have a heart attack at one point!' Jenny laughed at the memory.

'Oh gosh, yes, I do remember that now! And when we eventually left, she looked at us as if she wanted to kill us because we both just bought a pair of stockings. We were barely outside when we could hardly walk straight for laughing. Everyone in the street was staring at us as if we were mad. Gosh, I cannot believe that. It is coming back to me now.'

'She deserved the run around. That snooty comment she made when we walked in, do you remember that?'

She frowned at her friend and then she broke into a smile.

'Yes, of course! I remember now, she said – *are you two ladies in the right shop? I'm not sure we have the sort of thing you will be looking for* – that did it for us, we looked at each other and thought, well, we will have a damn good go trying to.'

They started to laugh at the memory.

'I knew this would be a good idea. I just needed a bit of a prompt in the right direction. What did we do then?'

'We went for tea at Betty's. Well, a rather late lunch. We decided we were in the mood to be ladies that lunch, so we decided to skip the usual place at Woolworths and enjoy a more luxurious atmosphere.'

'What time was that?'

'I can't exactly remember but it was getting on to be quite late in the afternoon. We had stopped earlier, shortly after we met and had a cup of tea and a biscuit and fed the babies, but they needed another feed. We decided to annoy more posh people and ask them to heat the bottles up for us. That backfired because they were just lovely. They couldn't do enough for us. The waitress was cooing all over the babies. Do you remember? She kept saying – *ah bless them, aren't they a bonnie pair, best days of your life* - is that the woman you remember talking to?'

'No, I don't think so. That memory seems familiar and yes,' she remembers excitedly, 'I do remember her; she brought us a selection of cakes and said that we could choose two each because they weren't open that much longer and they couldn't sell them the following day. She put an extra one in a box each for us to take home and didn't charge for them. Yes. I remember that! We walked over to the park and time ran away from us and it was ever so late because it was dark but we just didn't want the day to end. I remember we had to eventually call it a day as we both needed to get our last train home.'

She was getting excited as the memories flooded back. It didn't matter that she was unsure of the timeline because she was remembering that day and the bits of her fragmented memory were coming back.

The two women enjoyed the rest of their day together and she was pleased that she had made the effort to catch up with Jenny. The hardest part of the day was still to come though.

Bill had travelled into Leeds with her and left her there to meet her friend. He insisted that she should travel back alone on the train and face her demons. It would be the first time she had done that alone since the accident. As the time got nearer to leave her friend at the station, she became more anxious. Looking back, Jenny had probably known. As they parted, Jenny gave her one of her big hugs and put on her bossiest voice. It was the voice she remembered Jenny used to mimic their old P.E teacher Miss Davenport. *Come on now, best foot forward, nothing to worry about, just get on with it, soon be over with.* She hugged her back and went to get her train from a different platform with the promise that they would not leave it as long next time.

It was utterly ridiculous to feel this level of anxiety. She'd done this journey dozens of times in the past. All she had wanted to do was run away and find Jenny again and get her to come on the train with her. The station was heaving. She was taken aback by the sheer number of people rushing about around her; it was dizzying. On the platform people were huddled together and the cacophony of chatter was overwhelming as it reached her ears. The smell of food wafted over from the eating establishments in the station and her stomach rolled. Part of her almost wished that Bill would be standing somewhere amongst the crowd, having ignored his fierce determination to do this journey back on her own. He hadn't been there. Her palms were sweating. She had a sudden flash back to the day of the accident, standing on the platform. Just as this memory flooded back, the train had pulled into the station and the intercom announced its arrival. Passengers got off and pushed past the people waiting to get on the train for its return journey. As fast as the memory came, it went again.

The platform had started to clear. She was jostled by people moving past her in a rush to get a seat. She was forced to go with the flow of the crowd. Once on the train, her eyes had flitted from seat to seat, trying to decide where to sit. There wasn't much time to decide as the train was crowded and she became aware of people pushing behind her. She sat down on the next empty seat she saw; across from her was a young woman and businessman. She had to focus on the two people to try to slow her breathing and remind herself that the journey would soon be over. She tore her eyes away from them, looking out of the window. All too soon green fields flashed by as the train left the city behind and made its way towards the suburbs.

There was an overwhelming feeling trying to swallow her up, making her want to just get up and run to the safety of the platform, but it was long gone, so she fought it and tried to concentrate on the people around her. Some were smiling and chatting, some were reading, and none of them were aware of the danger she was feeling. She felt a little lightheaded, almost outside of herself. It was if she did not really exist. The businessman across from her loosened his tie and closed his eyes. She stared over at him, taking in each line and contour of his face, concentrating on the details of his clothing... anything that would take her mind away from where she was. The faceless voice gave announcements of the various stops the train was making. She shifted her gaze over to the woman sat directly across from her. The woman was reading but looked up and caught Carol's eye and smiled.

Another flashback. Another woman sitting opposite her on a train - a woman holding a baby. The same as she had been doing that day. The baby was distressed. The woman was not getting anywhere despite her efforts to rock her. The woman was clearly anxious. She'd felt sorry for her. Sophie was fast asleep, being as good as gold. The woman continued to pacify the child but it wasn't working. It was coming back to her. Other passengers were turning around, looking. Somebody was tutting. They'd started talking about sleepless nights and how hard being a mother was. She had offered to swap babies for a while to give the woman a break. Sometimes they were monkeys and immediately stopped crying for someone else. Maybe she could smell her milk. Was she feeding the baby herself? Her question appeared to make the woman uncomfortable, so she hadn't pressed the point.

The baby still wouldn't stop crying. Its cries were getting louder and more distressed. *Let her have a go love. She's right. Sometimes they calm down with a different set of hands.* An older woman that was sat next to her, leaning over to the woman with the crying baby to intervene. The woman with the crying baby looked harassed and close to tears. *Alright then. Just for a minute.* Carol had passed her sleeping baby to the older woman so she could take the crying child. *I'm Carol and that is Sophie.* She'd reached over and took the baby from the agitated women. *What's your name little one?*

The memory went and a roar filled her ears. Adrenaline pumped through her body as the memories of that day started flooding into her head too quickly. Taking that baby and what had happened next that fateful day. The memories were coming thick and fast now, as clear as day. A well-meaning stranger had intervened. It changed everything. The older woman, who had been sat next to her, probably had brought up a family of her own. The older woman thought she and Carol could help calm the crying baby. They had both had the feeling that the mother was tired and distressed and had wanted to help. Nothing had been said. It was instinctual. They each had felt the same thing. It was a random act of human kindness; they had tried to help the distressed mother.

All the other memories of that day started to tumble back into place. The pieces of the jigsaw were complete; they had come together as one clear picture. She *hadn't* been holding her Sophie at the time of the accident. She'd been holding another woman's child. She had been pacing up and down, rocking her from side to side. She'd gone into the next carriage towards the rear of the train, as much to try escape the tutting passengers, as well as to keep the mother calm. The woman seemed so grateful when she had last glanced over. She had been cradling Sophie, passed to her from the older woman. She was visibly calmer and Sophie was fine snuggled into a blanket the woman had been holding on her knee. There had been some sort of loud clank, reverberating through the train and the whole carriage shook and started to sway as the brakes, she thinks, were applied. She remembered throwing herself into the nearest seat and pulling the child into her with one hand and trying to hold on with the other, curling up as she lost her balance. That was the last thing she remembered until waking up in the hospital all those months later.

Carol was thrown back into the present. She felt herself dissolving as all the memories crowded in. She felt bile rise to her throat. Her whole life was a lie. Sophie's life was a lie. Where is Sophie? Who is the child she thought was Sophie? She felt cold but sweat was pouring in rivers down her back. She thought she was going to faint. The man opposite her has noticed.

'Are you alright, love? You don't look at all well?'

'I'm sorry, I don't feel so good. I'll be okay. Just give me a minute'

The man is helped now by the woman with the kind smile. They are concerned.

'What stop is yours, love? Is anyone meeting you?'

'It's Ripon. I'll be fine, honestly. It's just a little hot in here, that's all.' She tried to slow her breathing and calm down. She had to pull herself together. Tears were pooling in her eyes. She tried to swallow them down.

'The next stop is Ripon. We'll help you get off.'

Carol forced herself upright. 'It's kind of you both but I'm feeling a little better. Thank you so much. You've been very kind. My husband should be waiting for me.'

On shaking legs, she made it to the door of the train as it pulled into her station. She had to make sense of it all. She couldn't tell Bill, she just *couldn't*. But she had to find out what had happened to *her* Sophie. She had to figure out who the child was, that she had nurtured and loved as her own for the last few years. She staggered towards the exit as the train pulled away.

CHAPTER 30

Ailsa

Scotland
Nov 1996

AILSA WAS ARGUING with Max on the telephone.

'No. No Max, for the last time I'm not coming back. You can box all my stuff up. I will collect it in a couple of days. Do not try to lie your way out of this like you did the last time. I should never have believed you after my suspicions the first time. I knew my instincts about you were right. You and that man- eating spoilt witch…NO! NO! Don't dare tell me I'm being irrational. I could smell her in our flat. She left her bloody bra tucked under the bed for god's sake and it sure as hell wasn't my bra. My tits are not that bloody huge thank god! They'll be hanging round her waist in a few years, so enjoy them while you can. Fancied roughing it a bit did she? In that squalid place we called a home?'

She hadn't been back in Manchester for more than a few weeks. Max had spent more and more time at the studio or out late at night in client meetings. The oldest lie in the book. She'd gone to Macclesfield to catch up with an old university friend, arranging to stop over so they could have a few drinks. Max had taken full advantage of having the place to himself and had obviously made the most of it.

Suddenly, all the things that had niggled her about his manner and boyishness fell into place. He had wanted his cake and to eat it too. He had wanted her there in the background doing all the running around for the studio, all the designing, organizing the events. Doing the job that would have cost him a fortune if he had to pay for it. Having sex on tap, cooking and cleaning up after him. God, she'd been a fool. He had turned those big eyes on her, flattered her like the good little lady she had foolishly been. How had she not seen it? Whenever she'd challenged him, it was flattery or he'd make her laugh or make her out to be unreasonable. She had loved him and he had taken her for a fool. She was so angry that he'd manipulated her so well. The last year or so had all been one big lie as far as she was concerned. He couldn't have loved her if he could just shag another woman. There was no fooling herself this time; the evidence was all there. It wouldn't surprise her if Miss Big Tits had left her bra there on purpose, Ailsa had thought, just to make sure she had found it. Women like her enjoyed the power. Well, thank you, Christine; you have done me a favor. He is all yours now.

She stood by the phone she had slammed down on him, shaking with anger and hurt. All her thoughts were jumbling through her head at a hundred miles an hour. Ann, who had been standing a few yards away, came up behind her and quietly placed her hands around her daughter's small frame. Her body was stiff and shaking, but as she became aware of her mother, she let go and started to sob. It was this picture that Ewan walked in on. His daughter sobbing and his wife holding tight to her in case she slipped from her.

CHAPTER 31

Sophie

November
1996

SOPHIE WAS STANDING next to Stevie's desk, having passed some files, she had finished with, over to him, to be actioned.

'Please say you and Jason will come to Devon with me for Christmas? I just need my bestie around me. The atmosphere is going to be really heavy.'

'Sweetheart, it isn't that Jason and I don't want to come. It's just going to be awkward with knowing how poorly your mum is. Don't you want it to be a more private affair?'

'That's just the point really. I know it's going to be difficult. It's a massive ask but Mum and Gran may need people other than me, Dad and Gramps. It may lighten the atmosphere. It's just all so hard. I really am dreading it. Please say you will come.'

'I don't know Soph. I don't feel comfortable about it. I feel like we would be intruding. This may be your last Christmas together. You do realize that, don't you?'

'I could hardly forget it, could I? Gran thinks you are fabulous and there will be other people in Devon for Christmas as well. Ewan, Jon and Brenda's son, his wife Ann and their daughter will all be there. We will get to see them. Jon and Brenda always arrange to get together with Gran and Gramps at Christmas.'

'I think you are underestimating how emotional this Christmas is going to be for your folks, Sophie. Do you really think that they will want to socialize with me and Jason? I'm not sure they will. I think they would prefer it to be just you guys.'

'I know it may be hard. Perhaps I'm being selfish but I really want you there. I think it will help to lighten the atmosphere, really, I do. If there are any awkward moments when there are tears or hysterics, I promise you can disappear off with Jason to your room or a walk somewhere.'

'Oh Sophie, tears and hysterics don't bother me in the slightest. You are happy to be around me and Jason when we fall out. It's not that we don't want to support you. Think about it, we haven't even met your mum or dad. How do you think they will feel having to make cheerful conversation around a couple of strangers?'

'I'm positive they would be cool about it. It isn't as though we will be the only ones in the house. It's a B&B. You already said last week that you and Jason were cheesed off that your original plan of flying off somewhere had fallen through due to Jason's work commitments. Just run it past him, please.'

'Okay, okay, if it means you will stop looking at me with those lost puppy dog eyes, I will.'

Stevie threw his hands up in the air, giving up under the pressure of her pleas.

'Do not take that as a yes, though. Jason loves you to bits, and even though I think he would love it at Sand Banks, I don't want to assume.'

'I love you Stevie Connors. You are the best. Thank you.'

'Just hold up a minute missy. I want you to check it out with your family first, particularly your mum. OK?'

'OK.'

She wasn't going to let Stevie change his mind, so hurried back over to her own desk and called her mother.

'Mum, how are you today?'

'Not bad at all, just a little tired. How are things with you?'

'Good. I can't wait to finish work in a few weeks. I'm really looking forward to spending some time with you and Dad at Gran's.'

'That's good. Your dad and I are looking forward to it too. It's the drive I hate, so we're going to take things slowly and set off really early, before the traffic builds up. We want to be past Birmingham before eight thirty.'

'That's a good idea. It's lovely getting up in the dark and watching the dawn break.'

Sophie took a deep breath. 'The thing is, I was wondering if it would bother you if my friend Stevie and his partner came to stay at Sand Banks over Christmas. They had other plans which fell through and I thought it would be nice. Stevie came with me in the summer and really loved it.'

'Why should I mind? It is a B&B after all.'

'That's what I told Stevie. He thought you may feel uncomfortable at the idea, over-whelmed really.'

'I take it you told him about the tumor then?'

'I did, yes. Do you mind? He's a really close friend,' she asked gently.

'Not in the least. There is no point ignoring the fact. I'm sure it's not going to be the constant topic of conversation. So long as he is comfortable about being around a dying woman, then it's not a problem!'

'Mum! Don't say that. It sounds horrible.'

'I'm sorry love. I just find it difficult to ignore the facts of the matter. I shouldn't just come straight out and say it that way I suppose. Your dad has told me off a couple of times already for doing just that. It's just my way of dealing with it.'

'I suppose,' she said. 'You deal with it how you want. It's your illness. I didn't mean to sound judgmental.'

'You didn't. This is new to all of us. We're getting through it the best way we can. For me, it is about facing the facts. As long as I know you and your Dad are coping, then I can.'

'How is Dad?'

'Oh, fussing like mad, but he seems fine. He is doing well, considering. We both are. Now is there anything else because I have things I need to be getting on with?'

'No, nothing else. I'll talk to you tomorrow. Love you.'

'Love you, too.' With that, the phone went dead.

Stevie had wandered over to her desk and had been listening into her telephone conversation.

'You didn't waste any time did you, madam. I take it your mum was alright with the idea?'

'Yes, she was. You're going to ask Jason?'

'I said I would, didn't I? I will ask him tonight. I'm not going to put him on the spot whilst he is working. You are a very manipulative young woman, Sophie Woods,' Stevie told her in mock sternness, turning his back on her with a flourish.

'However, you know Jason, he can never say no to me. I have my ways to persuade him. I'll call you later on,' and with that, he turned around and gave her a wink.

CHAPTER 32

Devon

December 1996

JON AND BRENDA had been looking forward to Christmas Eve for weeks. Their son Ewan and his wife Ann had, at last, made a firm arrangement to spend the Christmas holidays with them. They had the added bonus of Ailsa, their granddaughter, coming to stay as well.

'Now don't put your foot in it, Jon, by asking Ailsa about boys. She's still smarting from her breakup with that Max.'

'I'm not gar gar yet old thing. I do have some finer moments. I promise not a word.'

'Oh, I think that's them now! Oh this is so lovely. Come on, get the door. They'll have their luggage.'

Brenda bustled her enormous hulk of a husband towards the main door of the pub. It was still early but it would be a busy day in the pub today. However, they had no intention of covering the bar; they had made arrangements to get the extra staff this year so they could take a back seat. They had just opened the door as Ailsa was getting the cases out of the boot with Ewan's help. Brenda let out a shriek, half in excitement and half in shock.

'Where has all your lovely hair gone?'

'Nice move old girl,' Jon whispered to his wife.

'Well just look at you, young Ailsa. You are the very picture of perfection and what a very lovely trendy haircut, my dear.'

'Thanks, I felt like a change. It isn't that different, just a bit shorter than my usual bob. Out with the old and in with the new, but I hadn't really thought it through. My neck is feeling the cold a bit more,' Ailsa laughed.

'Oh yes, very fetching, darling. It was just a surprise is all as I haven't seen you with it that short before.'

Brenda threw her arms around Ailsa and gave her a squeeze and then a slap on her bum. A habit Brenda had of doing with male or female alike. Brenda then threw her arms around her son's neck, grabbing each side of his face in both of her hands and pulling his head down for a multitude of kisses. Jon shook his head from side to side, laughing.

'Put the lad down, woman, and let him breath.'

Brenda dutifully let go and then pulled Ann in for a ginormous hug.

'I've been awake since 5.30am in excitement. It's so good to have you all here. Now come on, come in. We'll catch our death out here. Jon lovely, help with the cases. I bet you are all dying for a cup of tea.'

Jon picked up two overnight bags and Ewan picked up the third. They were all chatting excitedly as they entered the pub.

Two miles away, at Sandbanks, Carol and Bill were sat in her mother's lounge around a roaring fire, drinking tea. Sophie was driving down with Stevie and Jason and had set off a little later but were expected within the next hour. Jane informed her daughter that she had accepted an invitation for them all to eat at the Rope and Anchor that evening. Brenda and Jon had wanted them to meet their son and his family.

'Brenda is so thrilled about having her family over for Christmas that she is bubbling over with excitement. I didn't have the heart to refuse. That boy of hers is the apple of her eye. Such a shame his job as a police officer has meant that they have seen so little of him over the years. I do hope that this will be one of many visits they make to her, now that his career is slowing down. Brenda never complains but I think she feels a little shut out of his life.'

Carol couldn't help but smirk at her mother's comments about Brenda's son being distant. Jane had been much the same with her. It was funny how people viewed themselves and others. Still, at least they were together now. Time was more precious than ever right now. She wasn't going to spend time worrying over her past relationship with her mother. She had more pressing matters to deal with. Perhaps she should have dealt with matters sooner. Her stomach did a somersault at what lay ahead. Some things were easier to deal with than others but she had done her best. When the time came, she hoped that her family would cope. They would have a lot to deal with.

Carol had seen her solicitor and had tried to make things as clear as possible for them. The solicitor had in his care, some letters which her family would receive at the appropriate time. She would do anything to turn the clock back, she thought, not for the first time. She had made her choice and she was living her last few days dreading the consequences. It was cowardly, she knew, to just leave it all to be explained in letters. It had been hard carrying the burden of what she remembered that day. She had spent weeks in turmoil and had, more than once, nearly told Bill everything she had remembered. It had taken months of research to put together details of the survivors on the train that day and it had ended in more grief when she realised that no other baby had survived the accident. Her Sophie was gone. It was like grieving for the first time for the child she had lost. She couldn't bear to lose another. She had just closed the door on it all at that time. Continued to live a lie. They may think that she was wicked. She prayed they would understand, eventually. It was an impossible situation that she had found herself in. She had only ever loved and nurtured this child as any mother would. She couldn't bear to have her torn from her. In one sense she was relieved that the truth would come out and she wouldn't have to bear the pain of being judged.

CHAPTER 33

Devon

Christmas Eve 1996

'I THINK WE should build up an appetite and walk to the pub. That way we are forced to walk home and we don't need to worry about anyone being tempted to drive after a drink. You okay to walk old thing?' Joe was directing his question at Jane.

'Don't *old thing* me. I am perfectly capable of walking there and back. I think it's an excellent idea. Does that suit everyone else?'

Bill looked doubtful.

'If it's all the same to you, I'll drive? I can take two more in the back if anyone wants a lift. Carol and I may head off earlier than the rest of you.'

He looked protectively towards his wife. She smiled gratefully at him.

'Oh bloody... I'm a stupid sod. I was forgetting. Sorry Carol.'

Poor Joe looked mortified, remembering Carol's weakened state of health.

'Joe, it's fine. Don't stress. I know my limitations and, although in theory I would love a walk and a drink, in practice it just isn't happening.'

'Come on everyone, I will go with Gran, Mum and Dad. You lovely, strapping men can walk. It will only take you ten minutes anyway,' Sophie gave the boys a wink.

'Strapping men eh sweet cheeks, I'm not quite sure how to take that?'

Stevie sashayed out of the door and into the hallway to grab his and Jason's coats. Stevie, Jason and Joe made their way out first. Whilst Bill, Carol, Sophie and Jane grabbed some wine, locked up and headed to the car. It was only a few minutes up the road and they soon passed the boys, giving Sophie chance to do her royal wave at Stevie as they sped past. Stevie responded with his own royal wave which was far more dramatic for effect.

At the Rope and Anchor there was a table set in the dining room off to the left of the bar. The dining room was closed off, just for them, today. Brenda had done a lovely job of dressing the table as usual. It had a white linen cloth over it with red table settings. It had two large bowls, set on mirrors with garlands of holly and ivy around the base. They were set at each end of the table with a pillar candle burning in each. In the corner of the dining room was a large tree decked with an assortment of red and gold antique baubles. Fairy lights caught the glitter and sparkle on the baubles. Each place setting at the table had a large red and gold cracker for them each to pull. A roaring log fire was crackling away in the hearth at the centre of the room. It looked warm and intimate. The rest of the pub looked very festive and cheerful. The long, carved bar had more fairy lights attached to the underside, casting a glow into the rich dark wood. Glittered stars, in gold and red, were hanging from the low beams, making the taller patron duck slightly to avoid catching them. Another roaring fire was blazing in another fireplace to the left- hand side of the main pub. The bar area was already filling up with the locals and there was a rumble of voices and laughter with *The Pogues* playing festively in the background. There was a lovely atmosphere.

Jane directed them to the serving end of the bar, where Brenda and Jon were seated with a couple and a young woman around Sophie's age. As they approached, Jon rose from his chair, filling the space around him and forcing a group nearby to move further into the bar area, creating room for the new arrivals. Jon grabbed Jane into a scoop where she was swallowed up by his giant embrace.

'Lovely to see you Jane, and this must be your daughter, Carol, and I presume you are Bill? Lovely to see you again, Sophie. I can't believe we finally get to meet you all. Come and sit down and let me make the introductions. Presume Joe is on his way walking with the boys?'

'He is,' replied Jane, 'they should be here shortly. Joe is a little doddery on his feet these days but don't dare tell him I said that.'

Jon ushered Carol and Bill into some seats opposite to Ann and Ewan, and he seated Sophie next to Ailsa. Everyone was shaking hands and saying hellos. Jon was ordering drinks and the boys arrived as they were sipping on the first round.

'I can't believe you have started without us,' teased Stevie.

'Come on lads, let's get you sat down and I'll get you a drink.'

Joe found the boys' seats and went to the bar to get the drinks.

'Brenda, Jon, you remember Stevie, don't you? Well, this is his partner Jason,' said Sophie.

'We do indeed. This is my son, Ewan, and his wife, Ann, and their daughter, Ailsa. Quite a bunch of us tonight. It should be fun!' Brenda turned to her family and there were more exchanges of hellos and pleasantries.

'Well, Brenda if you've met Stevie you will know that he loves fun, but I'm the sensible one, so we shouldn't be too much of a handful tonight,' Jason teased.

'You're so cheeky. I am very reserved and I'm sure Brenda knows that. I'm very shy till I get to know people,' Stevie retorted. 'I behaved last time I met you, didn't I, Brenda?'

'That was my point, actually. This is your second visit here and your fun side may escape and make it large,' Jason poked Stevie in the side as he grinned at him.

'He behaved like the perfect gentleman, Jason. Besides, we don't do sensible in Devon. In fact, we are rather under-estimated in the fun department,' Brenda laughed, setting everyone else off.

The evening was going well; everyone seemed to get on and the conversation was flowing. They had moved into the dining area and were seated around the large table. Ailsa couldn't take her eyes off Sophie. This was the girl that she had almost collided with as she was leaving her local Deli a few months ago. It had taken Sophie a little longer to place Ailsa, but when she did, she had felt odd. It was such a small world.

Ailsa couldn't hold her thoughts to herself any longer as she was again struck by the eyes and something else familiar that she could not put into words.

'This may sound wacky Sophie, but didn't I see you a few months back, in a Deli in Manchester?'

'Do you know, I was thinking the same thing? I was wondering why you looked familiar.'

Sophie remembered it well. It was the day Mum and Dad had turned up at her flat to break the news about how ill her mum was.

'You live in Manchester too then?'

'I did,' Ailsa replied, 'It's a long story and it would be totally unfair to off load the tragedy of my love life on you right now. Maybe after a few more drinks. Suffice to say, I have moved back up to Scotland to my Mum and Dad's until I can find a new job and somewhere to live. The job in Manchester kind of came with the man and the two no longer go together.'

'I'm sorry to hear that. It may be of no consolation that I am going through a dry spell as well right now. In fact, I think they call it a drought,' Sophie grinned at her.

Ailsa laughed, and the girls chatted on for most of the evening.

Ann had been watching their exchange from across the table and marvelled at how animated they were together. Ailsa had always been easy to get along with but it was as though they had known each other for years. They even had a similar laugh and slight mannerisms that mirrored each other. It made her feel unsettled but she couldn't put her finger on what it was. Ann was struck again by Sophie's eyes and now that she was sat next to Ailsa, she couldn't deny that she'd not been mistaken the first time she had met the girl, about how alike they looked.

About an hour after they had eaten, Carol and Bill made their excuses to leave. Carol had only picked at her food and Sophie noticed she was looking very tired.

'I'll come with you both,' Sophie said.

'You will not, young lady. You stay with everyone else. I'm only going straight to bed,' Carol admonished her.

'Are you sure, Mum? I don't mind?'

'Of course she is,' Bill said. 'Stay and enjoy the evening. We will see you in the morning.'

'Thank you for a lovely evening, Brenda and Jon. It's been great to finally get to meet you. Mum and Dad have told us so much about you.'

Carol got up and bent to give her hosts a peck on the cheek. It was obvious she was struggling. Bill put his arm through hers protectively. Brenda beamed.

'Like-wise. Just be careful on the road going back. The lighting in these parts is not the best. Enjoy your day tomorrow.'

The evening carried on for another couple of hours. The boys got louder and louder, and funnier and funnier. Jane got, as she called it, a 'little tidily' and Sophie suggested that maybe it was time to call it a night for her. Sophie had enjoyed the evening but couldn't help but fret seeing her mother slowing down and getting weaker. She needed to get back and check on her. Sophie turned to Ailsa on her way out.

'Look, as you may have noticed, and probably heard, mum isn't very well right now. I honestly don't know what the future holds but here's my number.' Sophie pushed a piece of paper into Ailsa's hand.

'Call anytime and if I can help in any way with regards to offering you a place to crash if you get an interview in the Manchester area, just call. I can't promise I will be there, as I don't know when I will need to be with Mum, but the offers there. It is always good to have options. I've really enjoyed meeting you.'

'Yes. You too, Sophie. When things get a bit rough with your mum and you need someone to talk to, you call.' Ailsa took a pen from her bag and wrote her number on a napkin from the table.

'Brenda did mention your mum was quite ill, but it isn't the sort of thing to mention if you don't know the person that well. I'm ever so sorry.'

'It's difficult to know what to say even when you do know them. I am only just getting my head around the fact that it is only a matter of time, or at least I'm trying to. I'm still not sure if it has really sunk in. I can't imagine how we are going to get through the next few months.'

'I'm really sorry, for what it's worth. Take care.'

The girls both hugged. Ann watched on as they embraced. Something was still niggling away at her but she couldn't put her finger on what it was.

When the guests had gone and the pub had been closed, Brenda brought them through some hot chocolate. Ewan had gotten into the habit of having one before bed since he had lived with Ann, so he had asked for some.

'Thanks, Brenda and Jon. It was a fabulous night,' said Ann, sipping the hot drink.

'Yep, thanks, Mum. It was good,' Ewan echoed.

Ann turned to Ailsa, 'You looked to be getting on really well with Sophie. It was like you had known each other for years. She seems a really lovely girl.'

'I did, yes. We had loads of things in common. It's so sad about her mum. It must be serious as she said her mum is not going to get better from it. I can't imagine how hard that will be on them all.'

Brenda sighed, 'The poor woman has been diagnosed with an inoperable brain tumour. From what I can gather from Jane, she's never been well since the accident. Oh, not with what she has now. According to Jane there have been issues for a long time. Apparently, she was injured over twenty years ago and she had some sort of brain injury or trauma. Anyway, she has suffered from depression and all other manner of anxiety since Sophie was a baby. Jane feels convinced that even though it was all that time ago, it was somehow to blame for the tumour. There is no evidence, as far as they can see, but Jane is convinced. It seems that when Carol told her about the prognosis, she said she wasn't surprised. It was as though she had been expecting something like this for years.'

'That is so sad,' Ann said, 'how awful for them all. What sort of accident was she involved in?' She asked, before taking another sip of her hot chocolate.

'Some sort of rail accident. It was years ago. Near Leeds somewhere, I think. There was something about it on the news. It was quite a big accident. I think there were over thirty fatalities at the time.'

Brenda turned to her son, 'I doubt you would have known much about it back then, as it wasn't on your patch and I know you tended to be knee deep in whatever case you were in charge of which is why we didn't see much of you back then.'

Ann felt like she had been punched in the stomach and went cold; she looked over at Ewan with an unspoken question in her eyes. He hadn't told his parents about how they met. He probably wouldn't have told them about the loss of Susan either. He may be a brilliant policeman but he did not communicate with his parents or go into details about his personal life. He never had. The look he gave her was almost apologetic; she knew then, that indeed, he hadn't.

Ailsa was quiet. She looked at her Mother and then at Ewan and then back to her Mother. The colour had drained from Ann's face and she look very uncomfortable. Brenda must not have been told about her sister. Her statement had clearly taken her mum by surprise not that Brenda or Jon seemed to notice.

'You okay, Mum?'

Ann came out of her reverie and turned to Ailsa, 'Yes, of course.'

'Okay then. Well, I think I'm ready for bed, so I'll say goodnight.'

Ann pulled her into a fierce hug.

'Night, sweetie. See you in the morning. Sleep well.'

'Night all,' and with that, Ailsa went off to bed.

'I think I'll get off as well if that's okay. Leave you all to it,' said Ann. Then, she got up, giving each a kiss goodnight in turn and left them all downstairs.

Ann was in bed with the light off when Ewan came up. There was no way she wanted a conversation tonight. Her mind was whirling round and round, going over the events of the evening. For the first time in years, she had questions she had to have the answers to. The only thing was, she had no idea what the questions would be, or whom she would ask them to.

CHAPTER 34

Devon

Christmas day 1996

'IT'S BEEN SO lovely spending time with you all. I can't remember the last time Ewan spent Christmas with his father and me.'

Brenda had just made her and Ann a hot drink, having finished the last of the clearing up. Everyone else had gone up to bed, all a little tipsy and over fed from the huge amounts they had consumed over the day.

'I suppose, now that Ewan has got where he wants in the force, the pressure is off a little and you can spend more time together?'

'In the main that's true. There are still massive workloads and not enough hours. Some weeks are busier than others. It really depends on the case. Sometimes he can be working crazy hours. When he gets the bit between his teeth, he forgets he has a life outside the job. I guess that is pretty common for any good policeman.'

'Yes, but since you've been married, his father and I have noticed a big change in him. He seems more settled and content and at least we get the occasional visit instead of the odd phone call.'

'That's nice to hear. He has certainly brought peace to me and Ailsa. I don't know what we would have done without him. Even before we realized we had feelings for each other, he was of immense support for a long time after he really needed to be. It was beyond what could have been expected of him.'

Ann was hoping that Brenda would pick up on the inference she was making. It worked.

'He has never really gone into details about how you met. He was very vague about the circumstances. Only that you had met during the course of an investigation. He is so like his father in that way, keeping things close to his chest. Never been one to be open about his personal life or emotions.'

Ann was surprised as she found Ewan quite open about his feelings. However, she was aware that he didn't keep in touch with his parents as much as she thought he should. Even though there appeared to be affection between Ewan and his mother, there was a slight distance between him and his father. Brenda continued to elaborate.

'When John was in the R.A.F, we moved around rather a lot. Although we had tried for a second child, we weren't that lucky. I had numerous miscarriages in the early stages and it was a difficult time. By the time we had moved for a fourth time, it was having an effect on Ewan. There were no siblings. Any bonds he had started to form with children his own age got pulled apart when we had to move. We decided that it was best if Ewan went to boarding school. That way at least he would not be dragged from base to base and would be able to form some stable friendships. Perhaps it was selfish of me. I needed to get busy doing something to take my mind off wanting another child so badly. It was becoming an obsession and was very damaging. The doctors could find no reason why I couldn't go full term. At the time it seemed the right decision. I wonder sometimes if it was. Ewan became rather independent and, very often, wanted to spend his holidays with one of his chums. With his visits home being less frequent, his father and he didn't have the closest of father son bonds. Sad but that is what happened. They love each other dearly, I know, but I think they missed out on some important moments with each other. Of course, Ewan will always be my little boy. Perhaps if he had been schooled near to the base, he would have been suffocated by me.'

Ann smiled.

'We do what we think is best at the time, I suppose. There are bound to be what if's. I should know that more than anyone. You see, I met Ewan when he was put in charge of my child's disappearance.'

Her words were spoken in a quiet and measured voice. Brenda looked stunned.

'Disappearance? Whatever do you mean?'

Ann felt slightly uncomfortable at having now shocked Brenda in this manner.

'I haven't talked about this to anyone but Ewan for years; it was a terrible time in my life.'

Ann took a breath and looked over at Brenda who was sitting patiently, with a look of deep concern on her face.

'It is a long story and something that you said yesterday brought it back.'

Brenda gasped bringing her hand up to her mouth.

'Oh my, something I said?'

Ann took her hand.

'It really wasn't your fault; you couldn't have known the implications of what you said. The thing is, I had another child when Ailsa was just a little over a year old.'

Brenda listened carefully and without interruption as Ann spoke. The two women kept hold of each other's hands.

'We called her Susan and she was beautiful, perfect in fact. It was a freezing cold day. It was a split second decision that I made, to leave her snuggled up in her pram when I nipped into the post office to drop off a letter. I'd not been in there for more than a few minutes. I didn't think those few short minutes could be so devastating to my life. I came out and the pram was empty. I still feel sick when I think about it now. That feeling will never go. I had Ailsa in my arms. I don't remember much after that. I was swamped by this overwhelming panic. Well, to cut a long story short, the police were called and it was Ewan and another female officer who attended. They were the longest and most terrifying hours in my life. The inevitable knock came on the door and for one split second you think *thank god it's over. They must have found her* but then you see the expression on the face of the person at the door and it is just the start of something worse. It is an unimaginable pain which stops your heart. I can't honestly remember the exact words. I can only remember the pain they brought. Susan was dead. A stranger had taken her - a woman from the village, whose child had died a few months before. Depressed, I don't know, but she just took her. Then she got on a train and just left the village with my baby. We have no idea where she was going or what was going on in her head. She ended up on another train which was heading out from Leeds. It had been a cruel winter and there was ice on the tracks. Though whether this contributed to the crash, I'm not entirely sure. There was some sort of problem with a wheel axle, metal fatigue, which resulted in snapping or some such thing. I didn't really understand what the report meant. Top and bottom of it, it resulted in the train being derailed, and with it, so did my life.'

'Oh you poor girl, you poor, poor, girl. I'm so sorry. I had no idea at all. That is what you meant by something I said. It was that same terrible train accident. It must have given you a terrible shock to hear me just come out with all that about Carol last night.'

The realisation that came to Brenda was overwhelming.

'Now you listen to me. There is no way you could have known that something so terrible could happen. Gosh, how many times you take your eyes off them for just a few minutes. To leave her in her pram on a cold day is the most sensible thing to do. Darling, dear girl, you cannot blame yourself.'

Ann pulled away wiping the tears that had run silently down her face.

'That's the thing, Brenda. I do. Every day. Just one bad judgment and it cost so much. My husband Stu went downhill fast after that. He had always liked a drink and he just drank more and more. It was his way to cope with the pain. Things just got worse and worse. The more he drank the angrier he became. He sometimes didn't come home at all after work. When he did, I dreaded it. Then he lost his job, then another and another. It was a complete mess. In the middle of all of this was Ailsa. I was afraid for her and eventually asked him to go. It wasn't all that long after, that he went completely downhill. He was found dead in some dingy room he had been renting. He blamed me for her being taken. I saw it in his eyes every day.'

'I don't know your husband. I've met men like him, though. The drink is what they turn to in any crisis in their life. You said yourself he had always liked a drink and sometimes it's easier for drinkers to blame other people when things go wrong in their life. Sometimes darling, they use those things as an excuse for their drinking and subsequent behaviour. Who knows whether he would have ended up dead at some point in that room, despite the tragedy that took hold of all your lives? There will never be an answer. You cannot spend your life carrying that burden on your shoulders.'

'I know what you are saying makes sense, Brenda. Ewan tells me the same things. I think I would honestly have gone under without him. He's such a good man. I hope you know how much I love him?'

'Sincerely I do, darling girl. He loves you very much, too. That much I do know. I can see how happy he is. You wouldn't have gone under without him either. You must give yourself more credit. You have another beautiful daughter and you had to find the strength to cope with it all and you did. You are a strong woman. Do not forget it.'

'Thanks, Brenda. That means so much to me. I'm glad we have been able to talk like this. I hope I haven't spoilt the day for you.'

'Don't be ridiculous, of course you haven't. We're family. Families listen and support each other. That's the way I was brought up.'

'Can I ask you something before we go to bed Brenda?'

'Of course!'

'Was Carol alone on the train or was she with Bill and Sophie?'

'From what Jane told me, Bill was working away on the oil rigs at the time of the crash. It was just Carol and Sophie. Sophie was incredibly lucky that she came out of it all with hardly a scratch,' Brenda replied sadly.

Ann was quietly looking down at her hands. Her head was a swim with thoughts and emotions. Brenda stroked Ann's hand in a motherly soothing motion, aware of the impact her words inevitably would make on Ann.

'Life is so very cruel. One child dies, another doesn't. It seems so unfair. Knowing this must make you angry. It's opened up things for you all over again, I suppose?'

'I don't know what I feel, Brenda, to be truthful. It is just so hard and unsettling to have come face to face with someone else that was on that train. To be truthful, I have been asking *why my baby* for years now. It has set my mind into overdrive since last night. What I need is a good night's sleep.'

'I think it's what we both need darling girl,'

Brenda pulled Ann in for a big hug. Both women made their way up to their beds. Ann spent another restless night tossing and turning. Although it was good that Brenda and herself were able to chat after the others had gone to bed, it had done nothing to alleviate the anxiety she was feeling.

CHAPTER 35

Ann

Scotland
Feb 1997

WHEN ANN HAD returned home after their Christmas break in Devon, she had tried to settle back into some sort of routine and forget how she felt. It was impossible. So many questions were still running riot in her head. Strangely, after having told Ewan of her conversation with his mother Christmas night, he'd also looked troubled. They hadn't discussed it further until now. It was a normal early morning for them. Ewan was polishing his shoes for work and Ann was on her second cup of tea.

'Don't you think it is strange that we find out all these years later that there were two young babies on the train that day - one surviving and one not. Well, weird really, that we ended up even crossing paths all these years later with the family. I never thought about the other passengers at all,' Ann said.

'I wouldn't say it was strange love. There were a lot of people on that train, a lot of casualties, some of them children.'

'I didn't see her though, did I? I didn't identify her. What if it wasn't her body?'

The words came out of Ann's mouth before she had even realized she was going to say them.

'Bloody hell, Ann. Where did that come from?'

Ewan was so taken aback by her question that he dropped the brush he had been polishing his shoes with.

'Sophie looked so much like Ailsa; it got me thinking, that's all.'

'That's a lot of thinking, Ann. Based only, I may add, on a few similarities.'

Ewan's expression was worried.

'Why, love, after all this time, are you thinking like this? It isn't healthy.'

'I know it seems far-fetched. I just can't get Sophie out of my head. Can we at least try and get some information from somewhere, as to where she and Carol were seated on that train, also, where that woman was found with Susan?'

'It was a long time ago, love. I'm not sure.'

Ann interrupted him before he could finish.

'Please Ewan. I can't settle. I just have this really odd feeling. I never even thought to question anything before because it never occurred to me to do so. Mistakes can be made. They have proven that recently with D.N.A. It can lead to unsafe convictions. Surely, therefore, it's feasible that a mistake could have been made with the identification of my baby!'

'I'm not arguing that point, love. Think about it though? Why would another woman not realize she had the wrong baby and go ahead and bring it up without anybody close to her knowing?'

'Ewan for god's sake, think how it all started. Susie was taken by a woman so distraught by losing her own child, that she took mine.'

Ann rarely raised her voice but she was getting frustrated.

'Also, bear in mind that Carol's mother was miles away. Her husband was working away at the time of the accident and how many times do you hear men say all babies look alike?'

Ewan shook his head and moved to the chair next to her and sat down.

'Look,' he said, taking her face in his hands, 'I'll make some enquiries, just to put your mind at rest. I'm worried about you, imagining and hoping that a mistake was made. This really isn't healthy for you, or either of us. Remember the guys that do this sort of work are professionals. I have never known of a mistake of this nature to be made during the whole of my career.'

'I don't care what you say. Mistakes are made. I never saw her. I should have gone and seen her. Please Ewan, at least try and look into it.'

'I said I will, so I will, okay. Now just try and put it to the back of your mind till I can get some more detailed information.'

CHAPTER 36

Ewan

Scotland
Late Feb 1997

I T WAS A little over a week later that he received a report with a list of the fatalities, casualties and survivors in each of the carriages. Alice McDonald and baby Susan had been discovered in the Fourth carriage. Ewan was re-assured that there had been no mistake, when he saw that Carol and Sophie Woods had been rescued from the fifth carriage. Carol Woods, her daughter and one male, were the only survivors from that carriage. Maybe if they had been in the same carriage there was a slim chance but it just couldn't feasibly have happened. The report made for grim reading. There had been many fatalities and six children were amongst them, only one was a baby. Susan. Susan's blanket had been found with her, which Ann herself had identified. There wasn't enough doubt, given what he had found, to pursue the matter further. He dreaded telling Ann. She had been totally fixated on the girl since Christmas.

Building different scenarios in her head. He'd explained that even if it came about there was a chance of a mix-up, they would need permission for a D.N.A sample from Sophie herself. Should she refuse, they would have to apply to the courts. Ann had been adamant that she would cross that bridge if she came to it. As the evidence backed up that there hadn't been a mistake, the sooner he told her and she got used to the idea, the better. He took no pleasure in being right. Human errors can be made but not on this occasion it seemed.

CHAPTER 37

Sophie

March 1997

THE FUNERAL HAD gone as well as could be expected. What was she supposed to say to people every time they asked? Why did people ask how a funeral went? It was such a stupid question. Sophie was sat in her old bedroom, thinking about the last few weeks since Christmas. It had been truly horrendous. She'd quit her job to help her dad take care of her mum. The firm had been supportive and offered to keep her job open for her but couldn't keep paying her a salary. Sophie had lost all focus on anything to do with work, in any case. So she decided to quit and look for another job when everything was over. Over. It was such a final word.

Her mum's health had become very severe after she contracted a chest infection in the middle of January. By the beginning of February, she had lost a stone in weight, from her, already slight, frame. Confusion set in and long bouts of painful headaches and nausea ensued.

Towards the end of February, the doctor wanted her to go into a hospice but Bill and Sophie refused and insisted on looking after her from home. They had the support by way of daily visits from a Macmillan nurse who administered Carol's pain meds and supported them with their feelings of despair and fear. They had been incredible.

She took turns with her father to sit through the night with her mum. Neither of them wanted to leave her alone for one minute. Near to the end, she was in and out of consciousness. In the moments when she was more alert, she didn't make a lot of sense. Amongst her tears of pain, there would be apologies to Bill and herself, even to other people. *Tell them I'm sorry. I didn't know until it was too late...couldn't let her go... so sorry.* Sometimes she would smile and say how much she loved them and how happy she'd been. There were times when she would toss and turn and mumble incoherently in her deep sleep. The amount of time she slept got longer and longer and her breathing became louder and slower. Each time she took a long, low ragged breath, Sophie held her own until the next one came. Eventually, the last breath from her mum came and went.

They had been with her at the end. It had been peaceful. The Macmillan nurse had administered her pain meds at 10.00am that morning, after a long restless night. Her mum passed at 11.30am, just as a cloud moved, allowing a stream of sunshine to burst through the window.

Now it was 'over'. The funeral had been held, the tears cried. She was so tired and numb. There had been so many people there that she hadn't recognized. It was supposed to be for family and close friends. She guessed her mum had more friends than she'd thought. It was nice to see so many people there. Jenny, Olivia and her husband came. Vicki, their daughter and a childhood friend, accompanied them. Stevie and Jason had both been there. Jason had flown back from Madrid especially, cutting short his business meetings to support her. Ailsa, who she had only met at Christmas, was there also. Ailsa had travelled up with Brenda and Jon, her gran and gramps. It was so lovely they had made the effort.

Ailsa had been in touch at least once a week since they had met. Primarily, it had started out as a catch up but she always asked after her mum and how Sophie herself was coping. Their friendship seemed as comfortable as childhood pals; it was incredible they had known each other such a short time.

It was amazing how together her father seemed. It was only four days since the funeral and yet he was so calm in the face of such a loss. It was un-nerving. Then again, he'd always coped over the years with her mother's depressions and headaches; he was stronger than she gave him credit for.

This afternoon they'd gone to their family solicitors after receiving a call out of the blue. He had wanted to go on his own but the solicitor had insisted he needed to see them both. They'd been surprised to receive a letter that Carol had left with him some months before. Charles Clifford, a rather scruffy but efficient chap, was the solicitor that their parents had dealt with over the years on legal matters. He offered his condolences and informed them that occasionally letters were left with him to be passed on to family members. Carol had taken him into her confidence concerning her condition. Carol had left word with her close friend Olivia to contact him on the event of her death and let him know that he had to disburse these letters.

They had both gone to their respective rooms to read their letters; she had sat there for ten minutes, contemplating, when her father burst in without knocking. He looked like he had seen a ghost.

'Have you opened it yet?' He shouted.

'No! I was just about to. Why?'

'I've just read mine,' he whispered. 'I will be in the kitchen when you have finished... and Sophie, believe me, I swear to God I didn't know.'

Sophie was ripping open her letter as her father was already closing the door behind him.

My dearest darling Sophie,

This is the hardest, most painful thing that I have ever had to do. I am so sorry for the pain this will cause you. I hope to put right some wrongs and hope someday you and your father will forgive me, together with the other people I have hurt. Please don't hate me. This letter, I hope, will allow you to...

CHAPTER 38

Ann

Scotland
May 1997

ANN HAD FELT utterly empty and confused following her conversation with Ewan, some time ago now. It was irrational that she still harboured a sense that Sophie was her Susan. She had to try and move on as it wasn't doing her any good dwelling on things she couldn't change. For the first time in years her grief had taken a fresh hold on her.

Now Carol had died. Ailsa and Sophie had kept in touch since Christmas. She was glad that the girls had struck up a friendship. Sophie would need the support of good friends at a time like this. Her stomach turned over at the thought of that poor girl and what she was going through. She longed to give her a hug.

She was in the spare room going through the small box containing Susan's baby things. She had no idea why she kept torturing herself by going through it. The smell when she lifted the lid transformed her to a time when she held that small body to hers. There was a knock at the door. She sighed, closed the lid and left it on the bed to go answer it. Hopefully, it was not a cold caller; she really didn't have the strength for any pushy salesperson today. Grabbing the latch, she swung open the front door, ready to be polite but firm and get rid of whoever it was. Her knees nearly gave way from under her. Standing in front of her, was Sophie. Her heart felt like it had missed a beat. Her mouth opened but no words came out. Standing there, shaking, she did not know how to react.

'Hello, Ann. Is it alright if I come in?' Sophie looked awkward and pensive. Finding her voice, she stood back to let the girl in.

'Of course, please come in. This is a surprise. Is Ailsa expecting you?'

'No, she isn't. Actually, it is you I came to see.'

'You came to see me?'

Her reply was clumsy and wooden. It didn't sound right at all. She noticed Sophie's eyes were round and about to brim over with tears that she had obviously been holding back. They were puffy from either too little sleep, or many other tears that had been shed already. She led her through to the lounge, directing her to the sofa. The awkwardness she felt, hit her like a slap in the face. The child had just lost her mother. She had to put her own scrambled thoughts to the back of her mind.

She sat gently down next to Sophie and put her arm around her shoulder. There was something soothing for her, as she felt the girl slump into her and start to cry.

'Hush now, love. It's alright. You've been through a terrible time.'

'It's not just losing Mum. Can you read this? It may make some sense to you. Dad contacted Brenda for your address on a pretext. He couldn't face coming with me today, but I had to. I think you'll understand why.'

Sophie had pulled out an envelope from her bag and thrust it into her hand. Her hands were shaking as she read the letter and she started to cry, still taking in the words, as tears streamed down her face. The letter was slightly crumpled as if it had been read and re-read many times. Ann took her time re-reading the contents carefully a second time. With each word her heart slowly released the invisible tight band that had been wrapped around it for so long.

'Oh, sweetheart. I just knew from the minute I laid eyes on you at Christmas. When I found out that you had been on the same train. It seemed too much of a coincidence. You look so much like Ailsa. I tried to get answers from Ewan but it made no sense from the report. This makes it all clear now.'

Sophie had been sitting patiently in silence as Ann read the letter and digested its content.

'I don't know what to do. I'm so tied up in knots. I don't know who I am. I have so many questions and I'm so tired and Dad is too. I'm so angry Mum didn't tell me herself, sooner. It was as if she didn't trust me. Trust that I would still love her. It was cruel of her to keep the truth from me. It was cruel to all of us. I miss her. I want to talk about it all with her properly and she isn't here and I'm angry about that as well.'

'That is understandable.'

'I was so scared to come here today. I wasn't sure how you would react. Do you hate her?'

Ann wasn't quite sure how she felt at this precise moment. Her mind was in a whirlwind of emotions.

'I feel angry for all the lost years. To have you taken from me once was bad enough, but twice, well I'm not sure how I feel. I don't feel any hatred towards your mum, though.'

'Poor Dad. He doesn't even know where his real daughter is.'

'Well, that I can help with. His little girl is safe, sweetie. You can let your dad know that, at least. We have a beautiful spot in the local church under a fabulous big oak tree. I took care of her.'

She could feel Sophie shaking as she cried.

'In a strange way, your mum saved your life for me.'

Sophie couldn't get her words out properly. She was crying so hard now that her nose was blocked and her words were spoken between ragged intakes of breath.

'How...can...you...be so calm...and...nice? I'm so... angry.'

'I was angry. Still am about some things. I felt so cheated...right up until I opened the door just now. But seeing you standing there and reading this letter.... Well now we know the truth, we can all start to make sense of things. We can't turn back the clock. We have to move forward.'

The tears were now flowing down both their cheeks. She pulled her daughter close to her and breathed in the smell of her child. Her baby was home. She smelt so good. Familiar in a way only a mother could imagine and understand. Her beautiful little girl had come back to her.

'I loved my Mum so much...I feel so betrayed...everything she seemed to be was a...a lie!'

Sophie hiccupped.

'It's ok to feel cross and disappointed. You can still love your mum. Carol is still the same person that loved you to bits for all those years. Was a good mother to you. Maybe she did make a huge error of judgment but don't let that stop you loving her and spoiling the good memories.'

Sophie pulled away from Ann and looked at her in disbelief.

'Do you really believe that?'

'I do, yes. I'm not saying that I don't have all these conflicting emotions, the ones you are also having now, Sophie, but where will anger get us? I'm furious about not finding the truth out before now and sad I've missed out on so much of your life. I want to shout and scream about it but it will lessen over time. Your mum's not here to defend herself. She laid out her reasons for keeping quiet for so long in her letter. Love is such a powerful emotion. Especially the love for a child. It's so fierce and strong, so part of me understands why she was afraid to let go. I'm just so grateful that you are here now.'

They both heard a key in the front door. It was Ewan, having picked up Ailsa from the station. They were giggling and laughing all the way up the hall. Ewan came through the lounge door first and saw the two women side by side. He was shocked, not moving from where he stood in the doorway.

'Oh my God, Sophie, what are you doing here?' Squealed Ailsa impulsively when she saw Sophie sat next to her mum. Then stood slightly shocked as she took in the sombre mood of the two women.

Her mother held out her arm to beckon them both over to sit down with them.

'It's a long story, sweetie. Why don't you sit down next to us? It may take a while and it would help to read this letter from Sophie's mum. Ewan, you had better read it too. It will explain a lot. I knew I was right. A mother knows.'

My dearest darling Sophie,

This is the hardest, most painful thing I have ever had to do. I am so sorry for the pain this will cause you. I hope to put right some wrongs and hope someday you and your father will forgive me, together with the other people I have hurt. Please don't hate me. This letter, I hope, will allow you to have some understanding. As you know, we were involved in a serious train accident many years ago. This tragedy was life changing for so many people. At the time of the accident your father was working away on the rigs and we hadn't seen each other for weeks.

I hadn't seen your grandmother as she was busy with the Bed and Breakfast, despite her efforts to get away. They didn't realise the mistake that had been made in the identification process; they were none the wiser, as they hadn't seen you for weeks. They say babies can change considerably in a short time. Bear with me as this letter tries to explain what I understand had happened.

I had been out for a lovely lunch with a friend and was on the train home from Leeds rather later than originally planned. It had been such a cold day but all the same so enjoyable. I was glad, however, to get into the warmth of the train. As we were about to leave the station, another passenger jumped aboard. I remember thinking: 'gosh she is cutting it fine.' The woman also had a baby of a similar age. That baby, I much later realised, was you. The baby was very grizzly and despite everything she tried, you wouldn't settle. I tried to catch her eye several times, wanting to give her moral support and then I just took control. Sometimes babies can feel if the mother is stressed and someone else can calm them when the mother can't. It took a little persuasion from my-self and another female passenger but eventually she let me take you to let me try to calm you down, whilst the other woman trying to help, had taken my baby who was sleeping peacefully. I remember how alike you both looked. The same cute nose and curly dark hair. I had been pacing up and down with you and the other passengers were getting annoyed at the noise. I looked over and I saw that my baby was now calmly sleeping with the women, so I walked through to the next carriage to avoid their tutting and disapproving looks. The last thing I remembered was a terrible screaming noise and vibrating through the train, then nothing.

I awoke feeling confused and disorientated. I didn't remember anything. I had been out of it for weeks. I was told of the accident and that you were safe. I was in a lot of pain but they kept on dosing me up on pain killers and I would drift back off to sleep. All I wanted was to get home to you.

Eventually I was allowed home and although I was mending, I didn't feel myself. Everything felt different but I couldn't understand why. I had been told at the hospital that I had temporary amnesia. No one could have prepared me for how long it would take for all the pieces to fit together or for the devastating effect it would have on me when the full realisation of what had happened hit me. It wasn't merely a few months, but nearly 5 years later that my full memory of that day returned.

My beautiful baby girl was gone. I had someone else's beautiful child whom I had grown to love, allowed myself to love because I thought you were my own. I needed to know where my baby was. It was a nightmare that I felt unable to wake from.

I found out more details of the accident. There had only been one other baby around your age travelling that day and she had died at the scene. I was crippled with grief and I couldn't share it with anyone. I know I should have spoken out but I couldn't. I couldn't bear to lose you as well. So, I carried on. I loved you like you my own. You are my own. I never stopped loving you from the day I held you in my arms.

When the diagnosis came, I couldn't go without telling the truth. I hired a private investigator to track down your birth mother.

Fate moves in mysterious ways. I couldn't believe it at Christmas as we were introduced to her. I felt sure someone was going to stand up and say something. Nobody seemed to notice how frightened I was. I suppose everybody put it down to my illness.

I noticed she didn't take her eyes off you, or her daughter. Your mother is Ann and it appears you have a sister, Ailsa. You both look so alike. If I was in any doubt about the information provided, I wasn't then.

You need to find her if you can. You were a good daughter to me and I hope you are able to build a new relationship with her as strong as the one we have had. I know your father will be devastated. Be strong for one another. He was totally unaware of any of this. I swear. Please keep him close and look after him. I love you both so much.

Mum x

Ann,

I can only say I am so sorry at having delayed the return of your child. It was not deliberate, initially anyway. It was a long time before I realised the truth myself. I swear. I know this is so little to offer so late. Thank you for the gift you were unaware you gave to me. My time as her mum has been so precious. I know it was wrong and selfish not to let her go but I could not bear to lose her. These words I am sure can't make up for the time you have lost. I have no right to expect your forgiveness but hope, in the years to come, you will be able to find it in your heart to, at least, understand a little.

Ailsa, I am so sorry you were denied the chance to grow up with your sister. Judging by the way you two just slotted together last Christmas, I have no doubt you will make up for lost time. It is no consolation for the lost time but I hope also you may in time also understand.

Carol Woods.

EPILOGUE

IT WAS A warm sunny day - a rarity for Scotland. The Scottish Highlands were rich in colour with the shades of purple heather scattered amongst its lush green landscape. There were only a small group of family and friends gathered around the grave of a small child. A new headstone had been erected with a few simple words. They all agreed it was only fitting to put Carol's ashes in the resting place with her daughter. It had been a difficult and painful journey over the last twelve months, for all of them. There had been tears but no recriminations. They had worked together to try and understand that mistakes can happen. People make decisions and it can change the path of life in a remarkable way.

Now, gathered together under the comforting arms of the old Oak tree, they found that comfort and peace. They were thankful for the love and family they had. When everything had come out, some found it was all rather strange that they had all kept closely in touch. Some friends were shocked and some drifted. Most people were supportive and understanding.

Sophie and Ailsa had opened a small Art Gallery not far from Ann and Ewan's. Not only did they work together but they shared the small flat above it. The gallery was a roaring success and the girls were practically inseparable. They both felt that they had a lot of years to catch up on. Sunday was always a family day. The girls would rock up at their mother's for Sunday roast and the three women giggled endlessly about one thing or another, usually forcing Ewan out for his after dinner walk and a little peace.

Bill was in the process of packing up the home he had shared with Carol. He had decided to make the move to Scotland to be closer to his girl. He was a little nervous about making such a lifestyle change but was looking forward to a different, slower pace of life having retired. He had good savings and would rent until he found the right place. He'd even decided to get himself a dog to walk so he could explore the Scottish Highlands.

Ann was more peaceful and content than she had ever remembered being. Life was rich and full. Ewan had beaten himself up for a short while that he had been unable to check the details more thoroughly. Ann had persuaded him that the past could not be changed. There was a whole chain of events that had brought them to where they were today. They had each other and for all the sadness and loss of the past, they had to be grateful for the here and now.

The group moved slowly away from the graveside, and the shade of the Oak tree, and out into the warmth of the sunshine. Two sets of grandparents, two fathers, two sisters and one mother.

THE END

ABOUT THE AUTHOR

BELINDA DEAN, BORN in Manchester in 1961. Now enjoying retirement in Heaton Moor with her husband, she has finally found the time to get her novel on Amazon: *Platform 2*. Look out for her second novel, hopefully coming soon.

Lightning Source UK Ltd.
Milton Keynes UK
UKHW041312060921
390024UK00001B/8